THE OUTLAW'S DAUGHTER

Matt Holiday is riding a dangerous trail. With $20,000 in missing gold to find and gunfighter Frank Waverly searching for him, it seems unlikely the gold will ever be returned to the Butterfield Stage Company. And the most dangerous gun on the range belongs to the beautiful Serenity Waverly, Frank's daughter. Although she rides with Matt, he suspects that will last only as long as it takes them to recover the stolen gold . . .

C. J. Sommers

THE OUTLAW'S DAUGHTER

Complete and Unabridged

LINFORD
Leicester

First published in Great Britain in 2012 by
Robert Hale Limited
London

First Linford Edition
published 2014
by arrangement with
Robert Hale Limited
London

A catalogue record for this book is available
from the British Library.

ISBN 978–1–4448–1888–8

Published by
F. A. Thorpe (Publishing)
Anstey, Leicestershire

Set by Words & Graphics Ltd.
Anstey, Leicestershire
Printed and bound in Great Britain by
T. J. International Ltd., Padstow, Cornwall

This book is printed on acid-free paper

1

The day was bright, sunny. Across the West Texas plains to the north there was a curtain of dark clouds, but these had been there for days, and seemed content to hold back and let summer progress in a peaceful manner. Half-dozing in the mottled shade cast by the pecan grove where he had drawn up to rest himself and his buckskin horse, Matt Holiday lay propped up on one elbow, watching the slow silver progress of the river.

Across the river was a group of kids who had a trot-line stretched across the river, fishing for catfish. He had seen them take two relatively small fish from their hooks — five- or six-pounders, at a guess. Just now they were paying little attention to their line as they poked, shrieked, kicked and wrestled away the summer day.

He was far enough away to be unable to hear the sound of the horsemen approaching the boys. They came into his line of vision and he glanced that way. Four men, letting their horses walk toward the river. Traveling men on thirsty mounts, Holiday was thinking. He saw them pause by the boys and ask a few questions. The kids, for their part looked up in reverence at the mounted, armed men who had taken the time to talk to them. They were more used to being ignored by adults.

Holiday sat up, yawned, glanced at his horse which was still munching dispassionately at the scattered clumps of dry grass, and pulled off his hat to scratch his head. When he again looked at the group across the river, the horsemen were riding off toward the north. They had taken one of the boys with them. The kid, wearing a straw hat, a shirt cut off at the elbows and twill pants looked back at his fishing companions and waved his hands in a frantic gesture. There was nothing the

2

boys could do, so they simply stood staring after the riders.

Holiday got to his feet. It did not look to him as if the boy was riding away willingly. He could be totally wrong about what he had only half-observed: it could be that the boy, after being scolded, was being taken home by his angry father. Holiday didn't think so.

He thought he had just witnessed an abduction.

★   ★   ★

Holiday stood watching the northward-bound riders, the group of boys staring after them, then he walked to his buckskin, tightened the cinches on his saddle and swung aboard, his face set, eyes narrowed with concentration and from the glare of the sun. He kneed the buckskin horse toward the river. Starting down the bank he found the going slippery. Upon reaching the river, he walked the horse through sucking red mud. Apparently the river had receded lately and quickly. The river itself was cool silver and blue as it made its way southward toward the Gulf of Mexico. The horse went up to its belly in water, Holiday doing all he could to keep his stirruped boots up out of the flowing river. They reached the far bank and again made their way through deep, clinging mud, then they climbed the bank to where the three remaining boys stood watching.

'Hello,' Matt said, drawing up before them. No one answered. There were three of them — all redheaded. All with pug noses and freckles. Each wore a fraying straw hat. They stood together in a row as if they had been organized by height.

'What's happened here?' Holiday asked the tallest of the three. At his feet was a large bucket containing four catfish. The boy looked toward the bucket, avoiding Matt's eyes.

What were they afraid of? Perhaps, he thought, they had skipped school or their chores to come fishing. A little more sternly, he said:

'Look, boys, I was watching. Did those men steal your friend away?' Silence. 'Or was one of the men his father, an uncle, older brother?'

'Will don' have no father,' the middle-sized boy said without looking up.

'Does so,' the smallest of the three said. 'He just got locked up in jail.'

'I never seen him,' offered the middle boy.

'Well I did, at Will's house once before he got locked up,' the other persisted. The middle boy shrugged.

'If he's locked up, it's the same as having no father, isn't it? Besides, that wasn't Will's father, was it, Howard?'

'No, it wasn't,' the oldest boy said, breaking his silence. Matt addressed that boy now.

'Where does Will live? Somebody has to tell his people what happened. His mother? Does he have a mother?'

'Sure, everybody's got a mother! Mrs

Waverly is her name,' the middle boy said.

'Where's she live, then?' Holiday asked. 'I'll ride over and tell her what's happened.' And ask her a few questions of his own. For he had already known that the man who had taken Will was not his father. The boys seemed relieved that Matt Holiday was willing to deliver the bad news to Will's mother, leaving them out of the situation. Willingly, almost eagerly, they explained where Will's house was, though they argued among themselves about the easiest way to get there.

Holiday started his horse on along a roughly carved path toward the small collection of mostly adobe houses that lay on the outskirts of Bentley, Texas. Glancing back, he saw that the boys had picked up their fish and bucket and made a run for it. To the north the low dark clouds lay motionless above the foothills, their cast shadows staining the hills purple and blue.

He was of two minds about this.

Should he have just charged after the abductors and tried to take the boy away from them? There were four of them, and besides he could not have been sure at first that anything wrong had occurred; now he was, but now the men were gone, and charging wildly after them seemed to be the worst way to handle matters. He would have to find out what Mrs Waverly knew.

There were no names, no numbers painted on the houses or the gateposts, but with the help of the boys' directions, he was able to find the Waverly house. A small white adobe with a plastered porch addition, it rested in the center of a dry-grass lot, appearing deserted as if it and its inhabitants had simply surrendered to fate and the passage of time. There were blankets over the windows as curtains, a weather-grayed wooden box held four withered rose bushes. Beside the house was a clothes-line. Dangling from the lines, fluttering in the dry breeze, was the usual assortment of

7

household laundry. But none of it was men's clothing. Frank Waverly was being given his laundry by the state of Texas these days.

Matt Holiday approached the dilapidated house reluctantly. Waverly's wife had already taken a bad shock when Frank was arrested. Now it was Holiday's duty to inform the unhappy woman that her son had been snatched by persons unknown. He had ridden on much more pleasant errands in his time.

And on a few much, much worse. There was no place to tie up his horse, so he left the buckskin ground-hitched in front of the place. The animal was well-watered, well-fed. It was not the wandering sort, anyway. Matt took off his Stetson, wiped back his hair and approached the front door.

The door was open a few inches, probably to allow the breeze to circulate. There was the smell of cooking within — the strong odor of fried onions and what he thought was beef liver. He rapped twice on the doorsill and stood waiting, his eyes going northward to where the boy was now vanishing into the distances. Across the rutted road a goat bleated aggressively at Holiday as if he were an intruder occupying a part of its territory. Holiday knocked again, more determinedly. Still no one answered the door.

Not willing to depart, he nudged the door open more widely, using his boot toe, and called in. 'Hello! Anyone home!'

Despite signs of occupancy and the smells of cooking, there was still no answer. Holiday stepped into the house which was plain, sparsely decorated with Indian rugs scattered across the floor, some plain furniture and a crucifix suspended on the far wall. He called out again and this time drew a response.

The young-old woman, of the type that had not been long upon the plains, but long enough for the harsh land to have had time to wipe away hope and youth alike, stepped into the room, apparently from the kitchen, for she was wiping her hands on her apron. Her eyes were blue, startled, her motions birdlike, shy.

'Are you Will's mother?' Matt Holiday asked and watched the woman blanch, her knees seem to loosen.

'I'm Bertha Waverly.' Her eyes filled with sudden fear. 'What's happened? He's drowned, hasn't he? Drowned in the river over a few catfish?' Her hysteria was contained, but only by a great effort of will. Matt responded quickly.

'No, ma'am, he has not drowned. But there's something I must tell you. Please sit down.'

Nearly staggering, the woman made her way to a narrow, leather-bottomed chair where she arranged herself. Her pale, blue-veined hands were folded in her lap, her eyes were haunted, expecting no good news. Holiday thought that good news very seldom found its way to her door.

'What's happened, then?' she asked in a dry voice. She seemed already to expect the worst. Holding his hat in his hands, Matt told her, as gently as he could:

'Someone's taken your boy away. A bunch of men on horseback riding north. One of them may have been your husband.'

'Frank!' Her head wagged heavily, denying the possibility. 'He's in jail.'

'I know he is, or supposed to be. He may have broken out.'

'It couldn't have been Frank,' the woman insisted. 'He would have stopped by at least . . . ' Her voice faded as her confidence in that statement waned.

'It might not have been Frank Waverly,' Matt said, partly out of a wish to comfort the woman in her illusions. 'I only saw them from across the river, and I don't know Frank by sight in any case. I talked to three boys who were with Will. None of them knows Frank either, or at least they have not seen him for years.'

'What can I do?' the shrunken woman asked. Her thin graying hair was escaping from its roughly fashioned bun. Wispy tendrils of hair waved in the breeze coming through the doorway. Her watery eyes seemed to be focused on the crucifix on the wall.

'I am going to chase those men down,' Matt promised her. 'If I can, I'll bring Will home.'

'How can you . . . ?' her expression changed, her eyes narrowed. 'Who are you, mister? Why are you volunteering to help out? What's your business with my husband if it was Frank who took my son?'

Matt didn't answer. Instead he said, 'I'll give it my best, Mrs Waverly.'

She did not respond, did not have the chance to as an inner door opened and a young woman with a Henry repeating rifle in her hands emerged from the interior of the house.

'Why are you upsetting my mother?'

the girl demanded. She was tall, slender in the way of horsewomen, with dark flowing hair and eyes that appeared black in this light.

'That wasn't my intention,' Matt answered. 'She would have suffered more if Will just vanished and did not come home night after night.'

'Maybe,' the girl admitted. She stepped forward a few paces. She was young, as Matt had known, but he could not guess her age. She might have been sixteen, eighteen, twenty — he was not good at judging a woman's years. She said, 'You saw this happen and you did nothing to stop it?'

'I was across the river. There was nothing I could have done.'

'You could have gone after them,' the girl argued.

'I wasn't sure what I had witnessed, who was involved.'

'But you are now? Then why are you standing here doing nothing while they're getting away?'

'I'll follow them; I'll find them,' Matt

told her. The girl's eyes mocked him.

'How, Mr Busybody?' she demanded.

'Tracking them.'

'You're a good tracker, are you?'

'I'm fair. I've been known to track a man down.'

'In the rain?' the girl challenged. Matt glanced toward the door. Beyond it the sky held blue and clear.

'You didn't notice the clouds to the north?' she asked mockingly. 'They're not moving this way, but those men are riding toward them. With a purpose — once their tracks are wiped out by the rain, not a bloodhound or Comanche would be able to pick up their trail. You don't look to be either.'

'Serenity,' the old lady said, cautioning the girl. If this fiery young woman was named Serenity, someone had missed the mark wildly when christening her. 'He only wants to help.'

'Why?' Serenity asked skeptically. The old woman's eyes closed and she shook her head again.

'I don't know; I couldn't guess, but

any help is better than none at all.'

'Maybe it is, maybe it isn't,' the defiant girl muttered. 'Let's find out. Come on, mister, let's get after them, and now!'

Matt wanted no company on this, and he would have argued the point if Serenity hadn't already been halfway to the door, grabbing a rain slicker from the coat tree in the corner of the room. She shot a challenging look at Holiday and asked, 'You coming along or not?'

Matt could only nod. This was not proceeding the way he had planned. He said goodbye to the old woman, who was too absorbed in her own thoughts to respond, and followed Serenity into the glare of the afternoon sunlight.

'Wait right here. I've got to get my horse,' she said, striding away before he had time to answer. Watching her walk away, he considered riding off and leaving her, but it would have done no good: Serenity would certainly have been able to catch up with him along the trail. Instead he waited with impatient resignation.

Serenity returned within fifteen minutes, astride a leggy roan with three white stockings and an evil gleam in its eye to match Serenity's own.

Swinging aboard the buckskin horse, Matt said, 'If we ride back to the river, I'm pretty sure I can pick up their tracks easily enough.'

'That'll make for slow going, mister,' she said brusquely as she spun her horse. 'There's no need for any of that pokey stuff. I know where they're heading, and if we don't hit bad weather, we might even be able to beat them there!'

2

There was little enough time for talking as they rode on at a brisk pace across the plains, but plenty of that for conjecturing. Why was Serenity so certain that she knew where the men were headed? What was she to them? By now Matt was almost certain he knew who the men were, but how could Serenity seem so certain?

The land they crossed was mostly barren and rocky. Here and there were clumps of greasewood, stands of nopal cactus an occasional yucca, but the grass, what there was of it, was yellow and dry. It seemed a land unfit for anything, like much of the West Texas plains. Ahead the low dark clouds still hovered over the foothills, as if they had found a place to their liking and taken up residence there. The course the two riders now followed veered away from the river and it could no longer be seen or smelled. Given his choice Matt would have followed the river; water was scarce out here, and besides, that seemed to be the way the kidnappers would have chosen. Maybe that was one reason Serenity believed they might be able to outdistance the men toward their goal.

Wherever that might be. If she had led him astray, it would take a lot of backtracking even to have a hope of finding their trail again. And what if she was deliberately throwing Holiday off their trail?

Eventually, as they slowed their horses and Matt was able to make out the distant Guadalupe Mountains hunched low along the horizon, there was a chance to speak to the dark-haired, black-eyed girl.

'How far are we riding?' Matt asked.

'Maybe twenty more miles,' she replied without looking at him.

'Are you sure you know where they're headed?'

'I'm sure.'

'Serenity . . . are you Frank Waverly's daughter?'

She glanced his way, smiling faintly. The expression was soon gone. When she shook her head it was as if she wished to dislodge the smile. 'No. My father was Bertha's first husband.'

'I see. So Will is your — '

'He's my brother,' Serenity said sharply. 'My true brother. I don't like it when people call him my half-brother. It makes everything sound so . . . incomplete, somehow. He's never known a day in his life when I wasn't there for him. He's my brother, do you understand?'

Matt only nodded. He hadn't meant to rile the girl up.

★   ★   ★

They were much nearer to the hills now. Matt studied the shifting shadows of the clouds across the land. He could make out rain showers falling ahead.

Sunlight occasionally struck through the cloud cover, brilliantly illuminating the creases and folds of the hills.

'We're not far south of New Mexico,' Matt commented.

'No,' Serenity said as if she had lost interest in any further conversation.

They rode on silently for another mile before Matt ventured to speak again.

'Do you think you know the men who took your brother?'

'I only know a few who would trouble to do it. Only a few with a reason.'

Matt pondered that, although he had already decided that the chances of a gang of strangers abducting the boy were nil. What could they hope to gain from it? These men did have something to gain.

'Do you know their names?' Matt encouraged Serenity.

'Well, I didn't see them, did I?' she said irritably. She breathed in deeply and expelled her breath audibly. 'A big man named Braddock and another called Whiskey Pete — they would be among them. I wouldn't know who else they are riding with these days.'

'But not Frank Waverly?' Matt asked.

'Why would he do anything like that? Besides, as we told you, he's in jail.'

Is he? Matt thought, but did not say. Serenity was a clever girl, and she certainly had not told Matt everything she knew, but then perhaps he was asking the wrong questions. It was a matter of knowing how much to ask, how much he should let her know about his own interest in all of this. She was already suspicious, that was obvious. He couldn't reveal all that he himself knew. If he did, she was liable to make sure that they never reached their intended destination.

'Do you think we can actually beat them to where they're going?' Matt asked.

'They'll follow the river, as you must have figured out. This is a more direct route.'

To where?

'So long as it doesn't start to storm, we'll get there first,' Serenity said confidently.

★　★　★

An hour on they hit the skirt of the rain. It pelted them harmlessly at first, doing nothing more than settling the dust and glossing the coats of their horses. By the time Matt had struggled into his rain slicker and Serenity had donned hers, the rain was coming down in earnest, pummeling them so hard that it seemed like ice falling against their bodies. The buckshot blasts of wind-driven rain swirled in the canyons ahead, twisted across the plains and forced them to hunch their bodies defensively. Glancing back, Matt could still see the sunny desert behind them, through the mesh of the falling rain.

Where they rode all was dark and growing darker. The storm was an

intimidating force, swirling and twisting, drawing a dark veil across their
vision. The temperature must have
plummeted twenty degrees in a matter
of a few minutes, and it continued to
fall. It was impossible to talk above the
wind and the rush of rain, so Matt
followed blindly as Serenity led him
along a nearly hidden trail which
wound its way up into the hills. There
were scattered, stunted junipers along
their way, and these stood trembling in
the downpour like palsied old men.

Lightning struck not far away, and in
the following salvo of thunder the earth
trembled. Matt's buckskin horse, stolid
though it usually was, balked as the
lightning struck again, even nearer,
filling the air with the scent of ozone.
The day seemed suddenly sulphurous
and jumbled, a sort of hell in panic.
Except for the bone-chilling cold.

They topped a small ridge where the
trail bent sharply upward, and paused
there, long enough for Serenity to shout
above the slashing of the rainstorm.

'We go that way — you can just see it!' she called through the screen of rain separating them. Matt looked the way she was pointing and saw, through the mesh of rain, the water dripping from the brim of his hat, a group of structures ahead, huddled in the canyon bottom below where they sat their trembling horses.

They did not belong there. Hidden away in these hills, all of the buildings were low, laid out without regard to planning. It was if some giant's foot had crushed them. Now it seemed that the confusion of the storm and the water rushing down through the canyon depths must sweep the pitiful village away if the rains did not stop soon.

'Is that where we're going?' Matt shouted back above the rush of the wind, the muted sounds of more-distant thunder.

'We'd better, don't you think?' Serenity answered. 'We can't go on much further in this.' Matt acknowledged that. If she meant to climb higher into the hills, the weather and red, oozing mud underfoot prevented any attempt at following the trail any higher. 'Besides, the men we're following — if they've any sense at all — will be holed up there until the weather breaks.'

That was true. Any men caught out in this storm would make for the nearest shelter they could find.

'One thing,' Serenity shouted, leaning toward him. 'You should know that this is an outlaw town.'

Meaning that not only was it a place where outlaws sought sanctuary, but that they were the ones who made the rules, passed judgement with their guns and did as they pleased without fear of any outside interference or restrictions of law. Matt nodded, even though Serenity was looking away across the gray canyon where black clouds still roofed the day and could not see him.

Matt had dared to enter such isolated, usually hidden towns before. Every man in such places was wanted, armed and volatile. Gathering together for protection from the law, these sanctuaries, as rough and dangerous as any imagined place could be, sheltered the scum of the earth. No lawman was inclined to enter such refuges sheltering thieves, gamblers, rustlers and murderers.

Not any who wished to live.

Serenity seemed to have no compunction about riding into the town. Perhaps she believed the reputation of Frank Waverly was enough to shield her from harm. Maybe it was; there was a set of rules outside the civilized canon which men like this followed. This rough code of law, known only to the army of criminals who did abide by it, was impenetrable to outsiders, but surely enough outlaws had their own definitions of what behavior would not be tolerated among them. Men seem at all times, everywhere, to construct some basic forms of civilization for their own protection.

The code of the outlaws was beyond

Matt's understanding and knowledge. Serenity seemed unperturbed as she guided her roan down the winding canyon trail toward the outlaw town. She was a bold young woman, as Matt had observed. He only hoped that she knew what she was doing.

With any luck, he was thinking as he followed her down the trail through the sheeting rain, they would find the men they sought — Whiskey Pete, Big Bill Braddock and whoever else was riding with them — Frank Waverly himself? — and rescue the kid, take him home without gun play and violence.

But it would not work out that way. As soon as Matt Holiday was identified they would go to shooting. If Frank Waverly was here, he and Serenity had no right to take Will away from him, his own father. But Will was more of a concern to his sister than to Matt, he had to admit. This bunch had to be run down and finished off. He had not told this to Serenity, nor would he. Let her believe that Matt Holiday was the Good

Samaritan he was making himself out to be.

Oddly, Matt thought as he watched the girl ride ahead of him, her back straight, her hair damp, straggling from her hat in the downpour, he did not think he could bear to see the contempt in her black eyes when she learned the truth of things. Would she regard him as nothing more than a vulture, a betrayer?

The town was now before them as they reached the canyon bottom and splashed their way across the engorged creek toward the narrow shelf of land beyond. The hills rose around them now, their tips scythed by the low clouds. The town lay silent in the rainy gloom. From somewhere through the gloom of the day Matt heard a piano being energetically played. He wondered who would bother to bring a piano to this god-forsaken place. Probably it had been stolen from a passing caravan and someone had been amused enough by the idea of the sensation it would cause to haul it in over the hills.

The street was a dark wash of rain, the footing red mud. Beside them now, Matt could see faint, blurred lantern light behind curtained windows and hear the storm-muted sounds of laughter and cursing. No one was out walking the streets, however, as was to be expected on a night like this. The water streamed from Matt's Stetson in quick, beaded strands. He slowed his horse, wiped his eyes and said to Serenity,

'We need to find someplace to get out of this weather.'

'Stick with me,' she replied. He trailed her two blocks farther through the rain. She halted her own horse in front of a tilted, two-story building and pointed to the flaking sign above the double doors. 'Camelback Stables,' it said.

With Matt watching doubtfully, Serenity swung smoothly down from her saddle and opened one of the tall doors. Returning, she nodded and walked her roan into the interior of the weather-beaten building.

It was not completely dark inside the rank-smelling stable, and by the feeble glow of two wall-hung lanterns, Matt saw that they were not alone there. Two men lounged against the wall near by, a third sat on a nail keg, his rifle across his lap. Matt glanced at Serenity, but she seemed unsurprised. For his part, Matt hadn't seen an armed guard posted in a stable before, and he grew wary.

'What do you want?' the man with the rifle asked, rising. His tone was surly, his eyes hard and set.

'Dry place for our horses, as you could guess,' Matt answered. From the corner of his eyes he could see the other two men moving toward them. 'Where's the stableman?'

'Gone. As you should be,' the rifleman said. 'This is a private stable, stranger. You'll have to take your business somewhere else.'

'Like Dallas, maybe,' one of the other men said. It was meant as a joke, but no one smiled. Matt decided that these were men without humor. Their entire lives were devoted to staying alive. Everything else was a mere irritant. He thought about backing his horse, considered the possibility of drawing his gun. Serenity, however, seemed unworried.

She said to the man with the rifle, 'Aren't you Coyote Sam?'

The man seemed stuck for an answer. Probably it was only one of many monikers he had used in his time.

The men were now gathered more tightly around them. All had brutal faces, slashes for mouths. Only the rifleman, Coyote Sam, if that was his name, was clean-shaven.

'And what's your name, little girl?' Sam asked in a voice revealing some curiosity, and a lot of menace.

'You haven't seen me for a while, I know,' she said as the men closed in on her. 'My name is Serenity. Serenity Ann Waverly.'

All motion halted for an instant; glances were exchanged. The Waverly name seemed to be a good enough password. Matt was still uncertain, but Serenity was confident enough to swing down from the roan and lead it to a stall where she backed her horse, flipped a stirrup over and began undoing her cinch as if she had no concerns in the world. Matt was still mounted, but he figured he should follow suit before the men started to wonder who he was.

'Men I'm looking for,' Serenity called from the stall, 'are Whiskey Pete and Big Bill Braddock. They'll be riding with a couple of other men and a boy. Seen anything of them?'

'Whiskey Pete?' Coyote Sam said. 'Is he still around? I heard he got locked up down South.'

'He's around,' Serenity told him.

'Is your father . . . with them?'

'Still locked up,' Serenity said, tossing

her wet saddle over a rail. 'But he'll be out soon.'

'I haven't seen them,' Sam said. 'Have you, Lou? I expect the rain is holding them up.' There were questions in his eyes, but a man didn't ask many questions in a town like this.

'Now we need a dry place for ourselves,' Serenity said, standing with her hands on her hips, facing Sam. 'Does Myrna still have that boarding house?'

'No,' Sam said. 'I can tell you haven't been around for a while. Her old boyfriend, Mike Case, got the idea she had taken up with another man, and he burned her place down last year to teach her a lesson.'

'Try Deke's place,' the man called Lou said. 'It's pretty rough in the saloon, but he's got rooms upstairs that are mostly clean and neat.'

'As long as they're dry,' Serenity said, and now the men did smile, more to please her than in amusement, it seemed. She had decided to insert Matt in the role of a subordinate, it seemed. 'A man hired for trail protection,' she said as she brushed past him, 'Come along, Waco. Let's see what sort of accommodations we can find.'

Matt trailed after her obediently. The role provided him with some sort of bona fides for appearing in the outlaw town where he was unknown and likely to be challenged at some point. All men were suspect here unless they were known inside the community. He thought he had recognized the man called Coyote Sam, though that wasn't the name he was using when Matt had last encountered him. A long time ago, it was, and it had been only a trifling affair; he doubted Sam would recognize him.

What troubled Matt a little more was how many other men he might run into, men with whom he had had a more than nodding acquaintance, who would not take kindly to his presence. Oh well! That was all a part of the job, wasn't it?

As he waited outside the establishment known as Deke's, using the landing of the rickety stairs that led up to it for shelter, he watched Serenity confidently enter the building and return in a few minutes, displaying two room keys.

'Let's go on up,' she said, 'I've got to get out of these wet clothes.'

Upstairs they found a hallway which opened on to eight or nine different rooms. The carpet underfoot was rust-colored and threadbare. The doors looked as if they had never been painted, but once inside his room Matt found a neat arrangement of bed, mirror and wash basin, and a straight-backed chair. The wallpaper was faded, but he had never concerned himself much with wallpaper. Beyond the window the rain continued to stream down. Quicksilver rivulets of water raced down the panes.

With a sigh he sat on the bed and tugged off his sodden boots. They were soaked through and heavy with red mud, he saw unhappily. Well, morning was soon enough to worry about that. For now he was dry and fairly warm, though the hunger knotting his stomach had only increased. When the door opened behind him, he rose and spun.

'Jittery, aren't you?' Serenity asked, entering. She wore a deep-blue dressing-gown; her hair had been brushed out and seemed only a little damp. It was astonishing that she could have pulled herself together so quickly. Matt was aware of his wet jeans sticking to his cold body, the shuddering of his shoulders. He had almost no feeling in his toes. Serenity, meanwhile stood there tall and sleek and confident. Her dark eyes held a faint amusement for a few moments. Then they grew darker yet and confrontational.

'All right, mister,' she said, closing the door behind her. 'I think it's time we had an honest talk.'

3

'All right,' Matt said, 'I suppose you're right.' Hail racketed down against the roof for a few minutes, and then settled again to the constant swoosh of rain. 'How'd you know where this place was, and for that matter, where are we headed?'

'I used to come up to Camelback with my father now and then, when he had business to take care of,' Serenity said, seating herself in the wooden chair.

Collecting a gang, more than likely, Matt thought. Planning another job.

'As to where we're going, you'll see. It's a little hideaway my father and his . . . friends have up here.'

'Do you have any idea why your father's friends have snatched Will?' he asked. She hesitated. Her dark eyes met his, fell away and then returned. She was going to lie, he thought, and she did.

'No.'

'I wonder if they're here — Whiskey Pete, Braddock and Will?'

'Not yet,' Serenity told him. 'Maybe they've decided to go on to the hideout; maybe the rain has them pinned down somewhere. I had one of the girls — one of Deke's bar girls — take a quick look around downstairs. They might be in Camelback, but they're not at Deke's, not now.'

'You already have someone helping you?' Matt said in astonishment. 'How?'

'It's easy when you know the ropes,' Serenity said with a casual gesture. 'Where do you think I got this?' she plucked at the fabric of the dressing-gown she was wearing. 'Her name is Laura; she'll be bringing you some dry clothes after awhile.'

'Just like that?'

'A lot of people in this town owe Frank Waverly favors.'

Matt nodded his head. Serenity rose and he thought that she was about to leave. Instead she turned to face him, leaning slightly forward, and spoke sharply.

'This is supposed to be an honest talk, remember? How about you taking your turn at a little honesty, mister?'

Matt was cornered and he knew it. He didn't want to talk, but he could see no reasonable way of refusing without alienating the girl and losing her knowledge of the whereabouts of the hideout he was searching for. Her black eyes searched his, seared them and finally, with resignation he told her.

'I'm Matt Holiday,' he said, still seated on the bed, Serenity's cutting gaze still on him.

'And you wear a badge,' Serenity said with a hint of rising anger.

'No,' he said, holding up a hand, palm outward. 'I do not. What I am is a recovery agent for the Butterfield Stage Line. As you may or may not know, stage companies are paid insurance money to ensure the safe transfer of goods and merchandise on their line. When something doesn't reach its destination, it puts a big hole in the corporate pocket of Butterfield.'

Serenity, always impatient, interrupted sharply. 'You're still looking for that gold shipment.'

'I am. I'll look until I find it. That's how I make my living.'

Serenity paced the floor; she went to the window and looked out through the rain at the forlorn little town. She crossed the room again and stopped, glaring down at Matt.

'Frank Waverly had nothing to do with that stage holdup!'

'They sent him to jail over it.'

'He was innocent. He was just handy and his past record condemned him.'

'Maybe so,' Matt replied, meeting her savage gaze. 'I had nothing to do with that, and I'm not out here to arrest anyone — I haven't the authority. Besides, these men have already served their time. They couldn't be arrested and charged with the same crime a second time. My employers have a long memory, however; they still want that gold shipment recovered.'

'You were trailing Whiskey Pete and Braddock?'

'I was. I am. Since they were released.' Frank Waverly, accused of being the ringleader, had received a longer sentence, but Whiskey and Braddock were known to have been involved in the crime, and none of the missing money had shown up; none of the robbers had been willing to give it up in return for leniency.

The army payroll had been a large one — $20,000 according to Butterfield records. A $20,000 loss to the stage line, since they had assured its delivery.

'So Pete and Braddock are going back after the money — wherever it was stashed?' Serenity said.

'That's our assumption, yes.'

'But . . . ' Serenity was baffled; her forehead furrowed. 'What has Will to do with any of this?' she asked, spreading her hands.

'I don't know,' Matt admitted. 'Two possibilities occur to me — I've had a lot of time to think this over. Is it possible that Will's father might have told him where the money's hidden? Perhaps Frank took it and stashed it where it could not be found?'

'Frank Waverly was not involved in the robbery,' Serenity repeated with precise emphasis.

Matt did not respond. Let the girl have her convictions to cling to. But he did have to say: 'The more likely possibility to me is that the other members of the gang, knowing that Frank will be released soon, have decided to hold Will a captive until Frank reveals the location.'

'He was not even there!' Serenity said with rising frustration. Matt nodded. He did not have Serenity's faith in her father's innocence. Nothing else made any sense to him. He had to believe that Will was going to be kept prisoner until

Frank Waverly gave up the stolen gold.

'What would my father's share of the money be?' Serenity wondered, returning to the rain-streaked window. 'A quarter of it? Or would he have gotten more . . . ?'

'Nothing, if he was not involved, as you keep saying,' Matt commented sourly.

'Well, maybe I was wrong,' Serenity admitted, turning to lean against the wall, her arms folded. 'I mean — quit looking at me so — you saw the shape Mother is in, how she has to live. And it hasn't been easy with Frank being locked up these past few years. She could use some of the money.' She added hastily, 'Whether Frank was involved or not.'

'The law says he was,' Matt replied.

'Oh, the law,' she said dismissively. 'Even you can't believe it's always right.'

'I only believe that we have to have some system in place to try to administer justice,' Matt said, watching

43

Serenity's eyes. Did the gleam they held now reflect her true ambition: to grab a cut of the stolen money for herself? He hoped not.

'Aren't you forgetting about Will?' he asked.

'Of course not!' she spat. 'But the answer to everyone's problems is in the same place.'

'The hideout?'

'That's right, and that's why I'm continuing on.'

'So am I,' Matt responded quietly. 'One way or the other.'

Serenity started suddenly toward the door, and this time she proceeded out of the room and down the hall. Matt grinned humorlessly. Their honest talk had gotten them nowhere at all. Perhaps he would have been better off if he had just continued to lie to the girl.

A sound at his doorway brought his head around and sent his hand toward his holstered Colt. There was another woman standing there — a red-headed girl with a nicely rounded figure beneath the flowered robe she was wearing. She wore a silver and turquoise necklace. Folded over her arm was dry clothing. Matt rose and tried his best smile.

'Laura?' he asked. The girl nodded and gave him a hesitant smile in return.

'Yes.' She showed him the clothes. 'Deke had these sent up for you.'

'Just put them on the bed, would you?' Matt answered, aware again of how soaked through and cold he really was.

She nodded again and brushed past him. As she did so Matt smelled among the overlay of powder and perfume the scent of bacon and eggs. It reminded him of what his stomach had been telling him all along. He had to eat.

'Are they serving breakfast downstairs?'

'Why do you . . . oh, I still smell like bacon, is that it? No, I ate out in the kitchen — the smoke must be clinging to me.'

'Do you think I could get a bite down

there?' he asked Laura now stood in front of him, looking up with intense green eyes. She was a full head shorter than he was.

'I don't think you should go down there,' she said with some nervousness. 'You've made some men curious. I'll tell you what; I'll bring you up something to eat while you dry off and change. All right?' she asked, and this time her smile was full if cautious.

'Fine,' Matt said. 'Just pull the door shut on your way out, would you?'

With the girl gone, Matt unstuck his wet clothing from his flesh and dried off with the rough towel provided. As he did he thought about his options. He did not think Serenity wanted him to travel on with her, not now since she realized that Matt's intention was to find the gold and return it to the Butterfield Stage Line. She had shown too much interest in finding out what was in it for her. But he also felt obliged to find Will Waverly and get him back to his mother. If the boy wanted to go;

46

Matt had not gotten over the possibility that it was Frank Waverly who had collected the boy.

True, Waverly was supposed to be in jail still, but something might have changed since Matt last inquired; he might have made a break for it, although with only a few months to go on his sentence, that seemed unlikely.

That line of reasoning returned Matt to an earlier thought of his. If Whiskey Pete, Braddock and whoever else was riding with them knew that Waverly would soon be out of jail they might be holding the boy hostage to make sure that Waverly, who seemed to have hidden the loot from the stage hold-up, would be forced to share it with them.

Matt had gotten as far as buttoning up his trousers when there was a cautious tap on the door and Laura appeared with a plate of food and a cup of coffee.

'I had to bribe the cook,' she said pleasantly. 'Guess who gets to do the dishes after breakfast tomorrow?'

'I'm sorry to put you to any trouble,' Matt said.

'Ah, it's all right,' she said. 'It will give me a break from serving in the saloon. I swear I hate it there. If I had any way to get out of Camelback, I'd be gone.' She placed the coffee cup and food down on the bedside table and sighed audibly.

'Can't you just go?' Matt asked sympathetically.

'Where? After six months here, I have saved about enough money to buy a broken-down horse. But nowhere to ride it. It's a hard land out here for a single woman without money, as you must know.' Matt nodded. 'But if I don't get out soon, I'll lose my mind if not my soul.' Laura continued. 'Remember I told you that I took my meal in the kitchen? Do you know why I do that? It's the only place downstairs where I can get any peace. You try to eat sometime with men passing your table and groping at you! It doesn't do wonders for your dining experience.'

Matt could think of nothing to say to that. Some of these saloon girls must have a hell of a life; he'd never thought of it in that way before.

'Is there someone who can dry my clothes and clean my boots?' he asked. 'I'd be willing to pay.' He ran his hands down the too-tight yellow-checked shirt he had been given and the trousers which ended well above his ankles. Laura smiled as he did so.

'At least they're clean and dry, though they don't do much for you, I'll admit. I think I can find someone to iron your clothes. I can scrape the mud off your boots, wipe them clean and stand them beside the kitchen stove to dry.'

'I didn't mean for you to have to . . .' Matt began, but she shushed him.

'It's nothing, Mr . . . ?

'Holiday, Matt Holiday, although I'd appreciate it if you didn't spread my name around.'

'I won't. As for helping you out a little — it's a pleasure. You're the only man I've met all day who hasn't tried to make a grab at me.'

The eggs on Matt's plate — three of them — were still warm when he sat down to eat after Laura had gone, and with the rashers of crisp bacon provided, they went down easily, quieting his growling stomach's complaints.

That done, he stretched out on the bed without undressing or unmaking the bed. With his hands behind his head he stared at the stained ceiling and thought, but, as with all such problems, his thoughts only ran round in the same circles, so, knowing that solutions were impossible on this night, he let his eyes close. He fell into a light sleep, his pistol not far from his hand.

Matt thought it must be close to morning when, some time later, he woke up. He lay puzzling a while over what had brought him awake. He realized then that the rain had stopped; the constant drumming on the roof had ceased. Had the change in the weather roused him?

Then, as his mind cleared of night-fog, he heard impatient rapping at his door and knew it must have been going on for some time. Fisting his Colt he eased toward the door and opened it. In the lantern-lit hallway a narrow, effete-looking man with long gray sideburns stood with Matt's own clothes and his boots.

'Sorry,' Matt said, 'I was asleep.'

'That's where I'd like to be,' the man said, pushing the clothing and boots toward Matt. 'These things have been cluttering up my kitchen. My name's Deke. I own this place. A certain lady said you'd be needing these if you were traveling on with her.'

'Serenity?'

'I don't know the name of no one in this town, mister. Speaking of which, I don't know yours and don't want to. Especially not yours. People have been asking about you, and I don't like that. This woman said for you to meet her at the stable soon as you were dressed.'

'All right,' Matt said, still drowsy and uncertain as he took the clothing from Deke. 'I'll be going.'

'And mister,' Deke told him, 'I wish you'd do me the favor of leaving by the back stairs. I don't want any more trouble than I already have — and you don't belong in this town.'

Matt's clothes were dry. His boots had been scraped and brushed. He wondered if Laura had done all of that. As he stamped into his boots, Matt decided that the little man was right. Deke did not need any trouble, nor did he. Coyote Sam and the others he had met might have been speculating about who Matt was. For all he knew Big Bill Braddock and Whiskey Pete had dragged into Camelback overnight. He did not think now was the time to meet any of them.

Starting down the hallways he reached the back door. It had stopped raining outside, and a single star was visible through parting clouds. To the east there was the first gray promise of coming dawn. The streets were still dark, however, still thick with mud. Serenity must be eager to get started again on this morning; perhaps she had begun to develop a little gold fever.

As he made his way toward the stable a band of dawn pink was beginning to show above the eastern ridge. A few tattered remaining clouds caught the color. Besides these the sky was clearing nicely.

They hit him as he stepped into the stable, looking around for Serenity. The first man gave a roar like an uncaged beast, and Matt felt the heavy blow from a ham-sized fist as it slammed against his temple. Turning to meet his attacker, he was struck from behind. Someone had an axe handle or something like it. Matt saw it as a blur arcing toward his skull and he managed to move his head slightly away, but not enough for the club to miss. It glanced off his skull and ear before thudding against his shoulder with bone-numbing effect.

That sent Matt to his knees, and as he fell he grabbed the legs of a man in front of him, managing to throw this one off balance. It made no difference. The two standing over him rained blows on him, face, throat and shoulders. Matt curled up into a ball before one of them finished it off with a powerful kick to his head and the lights went out all over the world.

When he came to there was bright light seeping into the stable. He tried to sit up and failed. Pain knifed through his head and he almost fainted away. He had been dragged back into a horse stall for some reason not clear to him, and left there among the muck. Levering himself up into a sitting position he leaned against the plank partition of the stall and tried to sort out his thoughts.

Who had jumped him, and why? It was meant as a warning, of course; if they had meant to kill him he would be dead this minute. Someone meant to give him a message, but who? It could have been Coyote Sam, Lou and his other nameless pal from the night before, telling him that he was not welcome in Camelback. But why bother, since he was leaving anyway?

It could also be that Whiskey Pete and Big Bill Braddock had reached Camelback and were leaving a message that they did not want him on their trail. In this town anything was possible.

Where was Serenity, and why had she sent for him before the sun had even risen? *Was* it Serenity who had sent for him, or had it been just a trick to lure him to the stable? Matt sat holding his head. He was carefully avoiding the other possibility: that Serenity had arranged the beating herself now that she knew Matt was determined to return the stolen gold.

Unfortunately, this last possibility seemed the strongest.

One thing was certain: Serenity was

not going to meet him this morning. The sun beyond the stable walls was already high in the sky. If she had come to collect her roan horse, she could hardly have missed discovering Matt.

His head only slightly clearer, Matt Holiday lifted himself to his feet, gripping the partition to pull himself upright. He stayed where he was for a minute, fighting off dizziness and nausea. Encrusted blood covered his left ear and a part of his jaw. His head throbbed. Matt staggered, stumbled forward, searching for his saddle and horse. Matt was not a vindictive man by nature, but someone was going to pay for what they had done to him.

He was not quitting the trail until he had recovered the gold and returned young Will Waverly to his grieving mother. The next time they tried to take him out of the game, they would have to bring more than an axe handle for the job.

4

The river was rampaging down the canyon topped with dirty brown froth when Matt reached it. His buckskin horse was reluctant to attempt a crossing, and Matt didn't blame it. The dark hills surrounding the valley glistened with run-off water from the passing storm. Overhead the sky held clear and blue, still embroidered with patches of wind-shifted white clouds.

'Take the bridge,' someone with a young voice called out, and he turned in the saddle to see a boy of ten or twelve pointing upriver. Matt was a little surprised to see the kid — children were rare in such places.

'I didn't know there was one,' Matt answered. 'Thank you. How far is it?'

'Take the bridge,' the kid repeated and then ran away.

Matt smiled to himself, thinking how

foolish he must seem in the boy's mind. In his world everyone knew enough to take the bridge when it rained.

He found it as indicated, and it looked sturdy enough. The buckskin horse's hoofs rang against the sodden planks underfoot as they passed over the frothing river and reached the far side. Matt paused for a minute, glancing back at Camelback, but no one was pursuing him. Then, taking a course toward where he and Serenity had crossed over the river the night before, he eventually found the trail leading into the uplands.

Underfoot the earth was still slick, put passable. By the time he reached the fork he and Serenity had reached the night before, the diverging, steeper trail seemed safe enough to travel, though he was certain they had made the proper decision in not trying to follow it in the rain and darkness. Now, as he guided the buckskin upward along the twisting hillside trail, he began to watch for tracks in the mud. Serenity would certainly have continued this way if she were able.

For this way led to the fortune in gold.

The trail upward was a treacherous one even for the sure-footed buckskin. There were stretches of solid rock and then again they had to pass over streams of red mud. Nowhere had a horse left a firm imprint although Matt could tell that someone had ridden the trail since the rain had ceased. What good that did him he could not say. For all he knew, being a stranger to this area, the high trail was ridden by numbers of men.

Yet, somehow he did not think so.

Camelback was now only an assortment of matchbox-sized gray buildings far below. The river rushed on, taking on a silver sheen now that the sun rode high. The clouds had parted and dissipated, their work done, and a cool wind blew across the hilltops. Ahead, Matt could see nothing at all. Only the brush-covered hills which joined together and separated in confusion, lending no pattern to the landscape.

Then he did see something. Perhaps a mile distant he saw, or thought he saw, a thin curlicue of rising smoke. The wisp of dark color was no more definite than an uncertain artist's first struggling pencil stroke across his canvas, but it marked human habitation. It was another hour, following the winding trail down into a sheltered valley, before Matt was able to make out a makeshift cabin hidden near a stand of scraggly piñon pine trees. The structure rested on a narrow bench above the bottomlands. Rainwater still leaked from the soil there, forming a beard of moisture on the face of the bench.

Matt paused, considering. Anyone looking out from the cabin had already seen him as he crossed the valley. He was well within the reach of a rifle. So perhaps no one was looking, no one was expecting trouble. Perhaps this was not the outlaw hideout at all. There was no way of knowing.

It could also be that it was Frank Waverly's hideaway and some passers-by had reached it, found it empty and decided to shelter up there until the storm had ceased. He needed to get closer, but cautiously. He circled the building, climbing higher now where stands of Jeffries pine trees grew, and an occasional cedar. He could hear no sounds from the cabin or anywhere in the area. It was a silent isolated world up here. Perfect, he was thinking, for an outlaw hideout.

Distantly now he could make out the Guadalupe Mountains through the pines. Surprisingly, there were patches of snow on their flanks, glinting in the sun. It was the wrong time of year and far south for that sort of weather, but the storm had been colder and more powerful than was usually seen in this area.

Matt had three or four thoughts circling his mind. First, was this the hideout Serenity had described? Were any of the gang in residence? Was young

Will a prisoner here? Looking around as the buckskin made its way through the sparse timber toward the cabin below, Matt found himself wondering where the gold shipment might have been hidden, if Frank Waverly, for unknown reasons, had concealed it from the rest of his gang. In this tangle of hills, it could be anywhere, although certainly Waverly would have used a landmark he could not forget to mark its location.

A buried treasure too well concealed is of no use to anyone. From Captain Kidd to Blackbeard and the Lost Dutchman mine, men had learned that painful lesson. One tree looked much like another, one rock among thousands was not so distinct as it might have seemed at the time.

The obvious place to conceal the loot was inside the cabin, but the outlaws would certainly search there first; what did they care if they tore the place apart board by board so long as the gold was found? So Matt did not believe it was in the cabin itself. The thought came to him that over the four years the stagecoach robbers had been in jail the treasure could have been stumbled across by some lucky passing traveler.

Reaching the verge of the forest, Matt reined in his horse and sat studying the cabin below. Smoke still rose from an iron pipe to stain the sky. Was young Will Waverly a prisoner there? Matt's job concerned only the recovery of the Butterfield Stage gold, but he could not help but think of a frightened young man and of his badly shaken old mother who waited, praying for his return. If it came down to it, Matt knew he would trade off the gold for the boy's safe return. A meaningless notion, he knew: he had neither boy nor fortune to bargain with.

He eased the buckskin down the pineneedle-strewn hillside, again exposing himself as he moved out of the trees. If anyone was here, where were their horses?

He approached the house with

utmost caution. The wind gusted up the slope and a high cloud cast a long shadow across the side of the hill. All was fresh and cool and very dangerous.

★　★　★

Will Waverly sat up in the darkness of the root cellar, wrapping the blanket they had given him more tightly around his shoulders. He listened, looking up hopefully. He was certain that he had heard boot steps overhead, passing over the rough plank floor of the cabin. They had come back then. But as he sat listening, watching, no one made a move toward the trapdoor leading into the cellar. No one spoke. After a while the movement stopped and he thought he heard the door to the cabin being silently closed again.

He had no wish to see Whiskey Pete, Braddock, Hadley or John Quirt again, but the cold isolation of the root cellar seemed worse than their company.

He would not starve, at least, Will

considered. The cellar held burlap bags filled with potatoes, turnips and parsnips. These could be gnawed at and made into a filling if unappetizing meal, though he especially disliked parsnips. His mother had always added them to the stews she made and Will had always tried to avoid them.

He thought briefly, longingly of his mother. He wondered whether, at least, Ernie and his brothers had taken her some catfish to broil. Things had not been the same since the deputies had taken his father away. Mother had so little these days.

Whiskey Pete and Braddock had convinced Will that Frank Waverly had made his escape and that they were to take Will to meet him. Will had had his doubts, but the chance of finding his father had outweighed his skepticism. Enduring a long ride through the night storm, they had arrived here, but Frank Waverly was not there to meet his son. There had been no way for Will to escape then, and certainly none now.

He was a prisoner. The thought was almost enough to make him smile. Frank Waverly was down in prison, Will a captive in this god-forsaken place, taken by his father's so-called friends.

There was no way out. He had searched every inch of the place and tried desperately to lift the trapdoor in the floor above, but they had moved some heavy piece of furniture over it. Even if he could escape from the cellar, there was nothing to be done. He knew the sort of country that surrounded the place, and without even a horse, he would never make it out of the area before they rode him down.

Exactly why they had bothered to kidnap him was something Will did not really understand. The men had not spoken much as they rode the storm, of course, and the few muttered hints he had heard since did not make sense. He believed they were trying to draw Frank Waverly after them — and kill him?

If that was their plan, he hoped that it would fail, although there was no one in the world he wished to see more than his father.

They were treacherous men, of that he was certain, and their plan, whatever it was, intended Will and his father harm. Still convinced that someone had entered the cabin, he watched the cracks between the ill-fitting planks and strained to listen for any sound, but there was no motion, not a whisper of sound above the wind. Feeling small and futile, Will sat down again on a sack of last year's crop of potatoes and waited in the darkness, trying not to cry.

★   ★   ★

That was that, Matt Holiday thought — they were not here. Nor had he seen any signs of recent activity in the cabin. The smoke still rose faintly from the iron pipe, though the stove itself was cool to the touch. Whoever had been there was long gone. Perhaps the stove had been used by a traveler passing the night there. Whoever it was, he was gone now. There was no food to be found, equipment or stored goods, no further signs of occupation. If the members of the old Waverly gang had been forced by weather and darkness to hole up somewhere overnight, they might not have reached the place yet.

Assuming, of course, that this was the right cabin at all. His eyes briefly searched the pine-clad hills. There was not another structure to be seen, though there could have been fifty hidden in the hills.

He stepped down from the porch in front of the cabin and retrieved his horse. What now? His options were limited. Return to the trail and sit waiting for Serenity to make her appearance? Had she even started out this morning? Perhaps she was still in Camelback, having wasted her morning looking for Matt. It could also be that she had indicated a false trail to him the previous night and was now riding in another direction altogether. He was certain that she would not give up the hunt.

Returning to Camelback seemed both the most promising and most dangerous of his few choices. Whiskey Pete and Braddock could be there now with young Will Waverly in tow. Serenity could be waiting for him. But he had been made well aware that there was no welcome mat out for him in Camelback. His head still throbbed with the memory of the beating he had taken, and his ribs ached dully.

Where then?

He swung aboard the buckskin horse and started it back into the concealment of the timber.

He had reached the verge of the forest when the rifle shot, fired from a distance, thudded into a pine tree close at hand, spraying him and his horse with bark. The buckskin reared up in pain and bucked violently, sending Matt sprawling against the cold earth. He rolled behind the shelter of a large tree, pistol in his hand, awaiting a second shot.

None came. The day fell silent once more. There was only the chittering of squirrels in the trees and the squawks of blue jays. Matt did not move for long minutes, fearing there could be rifle sights fixed on him. His injured shoulder stiffened and complained; his head began its constant throbbing again. The breeze rustled the limbs of the tall trees, rubbing them one against the other.

Looking behind him, Matt could see no sign of his buckskin horse. The stinging bark had sent the faithful animal into a panic. He hoped that it had not run far, for whatever he was to do, he would need a horse under him.

He walked through the wind-chilled forest, searching for the horse. If he did not find the buckskin, he was in a very bad position, he knew. The ground beneath the trees was still damp, the fallen pine needles made sodden mats under his boots. He circled a large twin pine and stood with his hands on his hips, looking down the long slope ahead of him. He could not give up the search; he was virtually doomed if he did.

When he least expected it a voice called out, 'Are you looking for this?'

Serenity Waverly stepped from the shelter of the trees and met his gaze. She held her Henry rifle firmly in one hand. The other, he saw, held the reins to his buckskin horse.

Matt looked alternately at the big horse and the rifle in the dark-haired woman's hand. Then he looked into her black eyes which were unreadable.

'Thanks, I was about ready to give up.' He paused, looking at the rifle. 'Did you take a shot at me?'

'Of course not, why should I?' she answered indignantly. 'Matt, why did you leave me? I searched the town and couldn't find you anywhere.'

Briefly Matt told her about being waylaid in the stable. She seemed unconvinced despite the obvious signs of the recent beating on his face. 'I went over there to get my horse eventually and headed out alone,' Serenity said. 'I didn't see you there, although your buckskin was.'

'They dragged me back into a stall,' Matt answered. 'Hid me there.'

'Who?'

'I never saw who they were. I was thinking it had to be Coyote Sam and his friends.'

'They wouldn't do that — not to someone traveling with me.'

'All right, then it was Bill Braddock, Whiskey Pete and that bunch. They must have gotten to Camelback overnight.'

'If they were there, they left early — after making sure you weren't able to follow them.' Serenity took in a slow shallow breath and told Matt. 'I believe I saw the four of them earlier, over that ridge.' She pointed in the direction she meant. The wind drifted a long tendril of dark hair across her face.

'What were they doing?'

'I suppose looking in likely places

where Father might have stashed the stolen payroll.'

'I suppose . . . ' A thought cast a dark shadow over his mind. 'You said you saw the four of them. What about Will? Was he still with them?'

'No, he wasn't,' Serenity said. 'That's why I made my way back here. They must have left him in the cabin, unless they . . . '

'They wouldn't kill him, Serenity. Otherwise their whole reason for taking him in the first place makes no sense.'

'Which was what?'

'I told you before: Frank knows where the gold is hidden and they intend to use Will to force him to divulge its location.'

Now Serenity sighed. She answered, 'All right, I'm convinced. My father was with the gang, probably its leader, and he hid it so that he wouldn't have to share the proceeds of the hold-up. I'm stubborn, but you have me convinced. Nothing else makes sense.'

'Now,' Matt said, stepping near

enough to take the reins to his buckskin which seemed shamefaced at its behavior, 'where is Will? We have to find him while we have the chance — before the gang comes back.'

'He has to be in the cabin; there's no other place.'

'I was just down there; it's deserted.'

'It can't be,' Serenity insisted. 'Did you look in the cellar?'

'Cellar?'

'Of course! There's a root cellar beneath the cabin floor. Did you look there?'

'No. It didn't occur to me that such a rough cabin would have — '

'They used to spend long winter months in the place, Matt. There's a root cellar, all right. I once went down there with my father to collect some vegetables for a venison stew.'

'Then I'm a fool,' Matt said. 'We'd better get back there. I wonder why Will didn't call out?'

'How could he have known who you were? It could have been anyone, someone who would put him through even more torment.'

Matt nodded and swung aboard his horse as Serenity retrieved her roan. He felt like a fool, but perhaps it was not too late to make up for his foolishness. If Will was in the cellar, he would be certain to call out this time, once he heard his sister's voice. The gold they could worry about later. It seemed unlikely that Frank Waverly would have hidden the treasure in a spot known to the gang. Whiskey Pete and the others were more than likely just killing time while they waited for the return of Frank Waverly.

When that would be and what it would trigger was anyone's guess.

5

Will sat up from his uncomfortable bed among the stacked potato sacks and listened intently. They had come back. He heard boots scuffling across the plank floor above him. The darkness was deep where he sat, and he struggled to try to see some sign of movement. Then a voice unknown to him said, 'They moved the stove on top of the trap. Give me a hand and we'll move it.'

'Then it's certain he's down there,' another, much more familiar voice answered. Will almost wanted to cry out with gratitude. He called, but his voice came out as a strangled whisper.

'Serenity!'

It was enough. She heard him and replied, 'We're getting you out, Will.'

He could hear the sounds of the iron stove being scraped along the floor and he rose on wobbly legs to stare upward.

The opening of the trapdoor caused dust to sift down into his hopeful eyes. Then Serenity was there, peering down. Beside her was a man he did not know.

'Get up the ladder, and quick,' Serenity said with urgency. 'We don't know when they might come back.'

'Sis!' Will cried out, clambering up the wooden ladder. When he was within reach, hands stretched out and pulled him up to stand on the cabin floor.

'Are you all right?' Serenity asked, kneeling down in front of the boy.

'I'm OK, I guess. But, Sis, don't ever try to feed me another parsnip as long as I live.'

'Let's shift the stove back,' Matt said.

'It won't matter — they'll discover that he's gone soon enough.'

'Let's just do it,' Matt said more gruffly.

Together they slid the iron stove back over the trapdoor, adjusting the round iron chimney which had canted away from its vent.

'Now?' Serenity asked, puffing slightly

with the exertion.

'Now we get the hell out of here,' Matt snapped. 'And quick. That cellar could end up with three prisoners if we don't get a move on.'

'They wouldn't put me down there, not alive,' Serenity said, snatching up her Henry repeater.

'Even worse. Let's get going. My buckskin will carry double. Let's get into the forest and circle south.'

'Are you taking me home?' Will asked as they scurried toward the waiting horses. Matt and Serenity exchanged a glance.

'Not just yet,' Matt Holiday answered. He pulled the boy up to sit behind him on the buckskin.

They rode silently upslope and into the pines. Once inside the shadowed verge, Serenity asked, 'What are we to do with Will?'

'If we had another horse I'd be tempted to let him try making it home on his own. But we haven't. There's no choice, Serenity, we'll have to leave him in Camelback until we're finished with the job.'

'What job?' Will asked. No one answered the boy.

Serenity's eyes widened. 'Camelback? What sort of place is that for a twelve-year old boy?'

'It's better than a root cellar,' Matt answered, not happy with the solution himself. He saw no other way to manage things.

'I suppose,' Serenity said, ducking under the low branch of a pine tree, 'Laura might help us out. Will could hide out in her room for a little while.'

'If she'll agree, that's what we'll do.'

'Deke won't like it if he finds out.'

'I don't think Deke likes anything,' Matt said, 'with the exception of money. Laura will just have to make sure that no one sees Will.'

'It's a lot to ask of her.'

'It's a lot to ask of Will, moving from one hidy-hole to another, but I have no other suggestions to make. Do you?'

'No,' Serenity said. 'I suppose that's

the only way to go about it.'

'Why can't we just ride home?' Will asked with a hint of fear. 'Mother will be worried.'

'That has to wait a while,' Serenity said in a soothing voice that Matt had not heard her use before. 'There are other things to be taken care of.'

Will was silent for a while as they started downslope once more, his arms wrapped around Matt's waist. Then he asked, 'Is my father coming for me?'

'He doesn't know where you are,' Matt said. As far as he knew Frank Waverly was still locked up.

'Why did you ask that?' Serenity asked her brother.

'They think he's coming — those men. I heard them say that he was, and then they'd settle up with him.'

'I don't think they meant just now, so soon,' Serenity said, but the boy was adamant.

'I heard them talking, Sis. They meant right now, or at least pretty soon. And when my father finds out that they took me, he'll make them pay, all right?' The boy's face was set with determination and prideful faith in Frank Waverly's abilities. The kind of faith only a young boy can feel in his father.

They rode on then with very little conversation. Finding the head of the steep trail down toward the river, Matt studied it carefully, looking for fresh sign in the damp earth, but no horses had passed this way except for their own.

Matt could see the sun glinting off the surface of the river, which flowed more placidly now that the rain had ended. The ratty little town of Camelback could now be seen squatting along the river bank. He wondered how he had gotten himself into this, and more importantly how he was going to get out.

He had a boy and a woman to worry about, a quartet of robbers behind him, $20,000 in missing gold, an unwelcoming outlaw town ahead of him, and, possibly, the gunfighter, Frank Waverly on his trail.

He was not smiling when they crossed the wooden bridge and headed into Camelback as the sun began to lower itself beyond the far hills.

They made their way toward the rear of Deke's place, slipping through the shadows of gathering dusk. They followed a narrow, garbage-strewn alley. On the street beyond the buildings there was a raucous concert of profane taunts and bellowed curses. Wherever the outlaw town's residents had been hiding out during the storm, they had now emerged from their dens eager for a rowdy celebration.

As they passed an alleyway they saw two men engaged in a brawl, but the combatants did not look up or seem to notice them.

'The whiskey barrels are open,' Serenity commented drily.

'I didn't think they were ever closed — not in this town.'

When they reached the foot of the

outside staircase leading up to Deke's establishment Matt swung down, sinking inches into the goo left by the rainstorm. He could see lights upstairs, and a few more gleaming from across the street, but there were no windows near by for anyone to look out of. It seemed safe enough. He lifted Will from the back of the buckskin.

'I'll just take him upstairs,' Serenity said. 'I'll be right back.'

'I think I'd better go with you,' Matt said. 'This isn't exactly your ordinary hotel.'

It wasn't, for within they could hear the sounds of men cursing, shouting, of glass breaking. Upstairs a woman shrieked. Serenity nodded.

'All right, but let's get moving.'

Matt couldn't see what the hurry was. Night was settling fast; they would do no more traveling on this night. And there was nowhere, really, to go. He knotted the reins to the buckskin loosely to the rail and followed Serenity up the staircase. The sounds from Deke's saloon grew louder as they approached the doorway. As they reached the landing it seemed to grow to a low rumble beneath their feet. Matt remembered hearing none of this uproar the night before; maybe the rain had kept most of the wild boys at home, wherever that might be.

Serenity swung the back door open and stepped into the corridor, an uncertain Will at her side. They heard the shriek of a woman and as he stepped inside Matt saw a tall, broad-shouldered man, hatless, his face furious, banging his fists on a door, shouting to be let in.

'That's Laura's room!' Serenity said.

Matt was already past her, striding toward the red-faced, liquored-up man. On reaching him, Matt shouldered the man aside. The would-be intruder staggered back a few steps, ready to stumble, but he remained on his feet. His face was blurred by drink, his voice slurred.

'You back off, mister. I'm getting into that room.'

'Not this one, you aren't,' Matt said, holding his ground. 'Go on back downstairs and have yourself another drink — if you can make it without falling down.'

The red-faced man growled, 'A man shouldn't poke his nose in where it don't belong.'

'No,' Matt agreed. 'He shouldn't, and yours doesn't belong in this room.'

'I go where I like, friend,' the man answered, spittle now trickling across his lip.

'Not tonight,' Matt said. The drunk was wearing a gun, but he had shown no inclination to use it. Now, however, he did push up the cuffs of his shirt aggressively and take a step forward, fists bunched, head held low.

It didn't take much. Matt jabbed out with his left fist, catching bone in the drunk's nose. Matt followed up with a right cross and this one landed neatly on the shelf of the man's jaw. The drunk turned away, let his back slam against the wall and slowly slid to the floor into a sitting position. His eyes were open, but they showed only white.

Matt crouched down to remove the gun from the man's holster. Will Waverly was at his side, excited by the fight.

'You sure showed him!' the kid said.

'Will, you could have taken him. I've never yet seen a drunk who could put up a decent fight, though they always think they're fighters.'

'Here, what's going on!' a voice called from down the hall. It was Deke, approaching them with wary eyes and uncertain steps.

'This man was bothering me,' Serenity replied.

'Oh, it's you, Miss Waverly. I didn't know you'd come back.' Deke stood over the downed man, making 'tsk' sounds with his lips. 'That's Davey Gillette. I'll have him taken away.'

'Thank you,' Serenity said in a voice close to a purr. 'Is it all right if we use the same rooms for another night?'

'Anything for you, Miss Waverly,' Deke said eagerly, although it was obvious that he was not thrilled with the idea; those rooms had other uses, and the night was humming. However, Frank Waverly's name still carried a lot of weight in Camelback.

They waited, watching as Deke withdrew and then Serenity tapped on Laura's door. 'Laura, let us in!'

The door opened a few cautious inches and Laura peered out. 'Oh, it's you,' she breathed with relief. 'Come in! Who's this with you?' she asked, looking at young Will Waverly.

'It's my brother, Will.'

'Pleased to meet you,' Laura said with a smile. Her red hair was in disarray. She was clasping her dark-green wrapper together at the breast. Matt was clenching and unclenching his right hand. She looked at him. 'Did you get into a fight with Davey Gillette?'

'You could call it that, I suppose,'

Matt replied, finding a cushioned red chair to sit on.

'All afternoon he's been chasing me around,' Laura told them. 'I swear, if it kills me, I'm going to find a way to get out of this rathole of a town!'

'How'd you get here?' Will asked eagerly. He was fond of the stories grown-ups told. The boys he kept company with had little of interest to say. Laura smiled at him. She went to the dressing-table and picked up a brush which she ran through her hair as she spoke.

'I wasn't much older than you,' she told Will Waverly, 'when my father brought me here. He was looking for men to help him with a job . . . of some kind. He left me here while the men rode off to take care of business. He never came back,' she said.

Will Waverly could understand that sort of story quite well. They never knew if his father would be coming back when he rode off. That was what had made his mother age so early in life, he thought — the worry. But at least Will had had a home to stay in while Frank Waverly was away. He felt suddenly sorry for this grown woman, and felt a strong kinship with her.

Laura tossed the hairbrush aside and regained her smile. 'You all must be hungry if you've been on the trail all day. The cook has a nice brown-gravy stew simmering in the kitchen, and I'm pretty sure I smelled cornbread baking. Who's ready for supper?'

'That stew don't have no parsnips in it, does it?' Will asked.

'Will!' Serenity scolded. 'If it does you can pick them out. Be grateful for the offer.'

'I could eat a bowl or two myself,' Matt said. He had been watching Will and Laura as they talked. Now he was looking only at the red-headed girl. Laura seemed to feel it. She tugged at the shoulder of her wrapper, pulling it higher and told them:

'Let me get dressed and I'll go down and order some food for us.'

'Want me to go?' Matt volunteered.

'No, I think not. Davey Gillette isn't much, but he has friends in this town. He might be looking for you. I'll be fine. The cook is a friend of mine and he has a meat cleaver.'

'Then maybe I'd better get back to the other room,' Matt said. 'Will, I think you'd better come along with me if the lady wants to change her clothes.'

'What about the horses?' Serenity asked.

'You're right. All right, then,' Matt replied, 'I'll leave Will in my room and take them across to the stable.'

'I can help with the horses,' Will said. He was beginning to feel left out of things, Matt thought.

'I think not,' Matt Holiday answered, glancing at Serenity. 'I've had a little trouble at that stable before.'

'You seem to have trouble everywhere you go,' Will commented.

'Go on along,' Serenity told them. 'Laura and I have another matter to discuss in private. When Matt gets back we'll all have a nice warm supper.'

Matt didn't know if Laura would be willing to take on the task of watching Will while he and Serenity went gold-hunting, but that was something he had to leave in Serenity's hands. For the time being Matt escorted Will to the room he had used the night before. It had been straightened up: there were clean sheets and fresh water for the wash basin. He left an uncomfortable-looking Will to his own devices while he went out again to see to the horses.

The night was cold, dark and rowdy. Someone had decided to sit down and attack the piano. It sounded as if he was playing with mittens on his hands. Matt gathered up the reins to the two horses and walked them slowly across the muddy street toward the Camelback stable. A place where, as he had told Will, he had not had much luck. If it had been Whiskey Pete and his friends who had beaten him, they were long gone now, hiding out in the cabin. Serenity was sure that her father's friends, Coyote Sam and the others, would not have done it, seeing that he was traveling under her protection, as it were.

It could be that the men who had beaten him were strangers to him, doing it strictly for their own amusement; it was that kind of town.

But when Matt entered the dimly lit stable again, he now carried his Colt revolver loosely in his hand and his eyes were alert for any threatening movement. There was no sound, only the steady clopping of the horses' hoofs. Matt stayed them for a moment and searched the interior with his eyes.

He saw the shadowed figure of a man sitting on a tool chest, slumped against the wall. His eyes flickered open, catching lantern light as Matt watched. Then he uncoiled himself from the chest and stretched his arms overhead. Matt did not know him, but he knew the type by his age and dress, by the old Remington revolver slung around his bony hips.

An outlaw, comfortable in this town, but one who had ridden many miles in his time and had now reached trail's end and waited drunkenly for one more chance at fortune which would never come, or for death which could not be far away.

'You want something?' the man asked in a whiskey-cracked voice in a manner that suggested that at other times, in other places, men had feared his challenge. Old habits, even those time has eroded, are difficult to put aside.

The man stepped forward into better illumination and Matt was able to study the scrawny outlaw. He was over six feet tall, but with a body that had been trimmed by age. His hand rested uneasily near his pistol. Suspenders held up his baggy pants. There were two teeth missing in front. He was, Matt decided, the kind of man who might be dangerous just because he once had been considered so.

'My name's Elias Foss,' the old man said. 'I expect you've heard of me.'

'No, sir. I'm kind of new to these parts,' Matt answered.

'Who are you and what are you doing here?' Foss asked with a hint of belligerence.

'I'm called Waco,' Matt said, remembering the name Serenity had used when introducing him to Coyote Sam and his friends. 'I just brought these two ponies over for Miss Waverly,' Matt said. He had not yet holstered his gun.

'Waverly?' The old man squinted into the light of the lantern hanging on the wall behind Matt Holiday. 'You don't mean Frank Waverly has a daughter?'

'I do. She's passing through Camelback and decided to stop for the night.'

'You don't tell me,' the old man said, relaxing visibly. 'How is young Frank these days?'

'Doing a prison sentence still, but he should be out soon.'

The old man chuckled, 'Well, Frank was due to get caught one of these times. Me and him rode many a trail and didn't get caught but once.'

94

'Well, it's a hard life,' Matt said, not knowing what else to say. He began unfastening the cinches on the saddles. The old man crept closer, perhaps needing to contact his glorious past in some way.

'What did they get him on?'

'Butterfield gold shipment job,' Matt said, trying to answer as he imagined a fellow outlaw would. 'Him and Whiskey Pete, Bill Braddock.'

'Whiskey Pete?' the old man scratched at his stubbled chin. 'Don't think I ever met up with him — after my time, I suppose. Big Bill Braddock I have run into here and there. Know him, do you?'

'I never have made his acquaintance,' Matt said, swinging his saddle up onto the stall partition beside him.

'Seen him beat a man to death down along the Smoky River. He was a bearish man then, probably still is. His neck swells out beyond his ears and his arms are as thick and strong as oak logs ... and that's no exaggeration, though people do sometimes build a man up for the sake of their story. With Bill it's just the truth.'

'How did Frank get along with him?' Matt asked, stripping the saddle from Serenity's roan.

'I couldn't say. The two never rode together back when I was around.' The old-timer squinted at Matt in the thin light the lantern offered, his face serious. 'But, mister, Frank Waverly could always take care of himself, take care of himself better than any man I ever run across. Bill would've known better than to cross Frank Waverly.'

Until now. Or was it that Bill Braddock figured that Waverly had crossed him, taking the gold and hiding it away from his accomplices?

Matt only knew Waverly from his arrest record, but every time his name was brought up men paid attention. He knew that he himself did not ever want to cross Frank Waverly's path; knew that it was inevitable on the trail he was following.

6

They had saved him a bowl of beef stew. Will had finished his and was devouring buttered cornbread and milk. Serenity looked sated and content. Laura was eating as well, but there was trouble in her eyes.

'What are you thinking?' young Will Waverly asked her more directly than Matt would have. 'You still look unhappy.'

'It's nothing,' Laura said with a shallow smile. 'Only my constant worry — how to get out of here, where to go, how to make a living wherever I might land.'

'Your father . . . ?' Matt began and Laura placed her bowl aside.

'My father's name was Ben Kennedy — maybe you've heard of him.' Matt nodded. If the others hadn't, he certainly knew of Kennedy, if only by reputation. He was said to be a gun hawk and the leader of a wild bunch. Shot down in Alamosa, they said.

'He brought me here, as I've told you. Stashed me, as it were, while he went off on one last fortune hunt. He promised me that when he came back we would buy the little ranch he always had promised me and that we would . . . ' Laura stumbled to a halt. Her eyes were damp and she did not wish to go on.

'Same thing with us,' young Will Waverly spoke up without inhibitions. 'Me and Serenity that is. I guess you know our father, Frank Waverly. Well he went off to 'go to work', as he always said when he was leaving. He never came back the last time. Though he's not dead. They just put him in jail and he'll be out soon. At least we've got Mother. I guess you . . . '

'My mother died years ago. I hardly knew her,' Laura answered. 'There was always just me and Dad. The men in this town used to be real respectful of me,' she said, looking directly at Serenity, 'until they learned that Ben Kennedy had been killed in a bank down in Alamosa. Things began to change then, slowly at first; later I had no protection here — I was no longer an outlaw's daughter, but only a girl nobody wanted to take care of.'

Serenity and Will did not reply. Their situations, Matt decided, were not quite the same. Serenity and Will still had their hopes, their invisible but still menacing, implacable father and his reputation to protect them. Laura had . . . Laura had nothing. Matt felt pity growing in his heart, but there was nothing he could do for the woman. Nothing at all.

'So, I guess you'll be staying with me for a little while,' Laura said to Will.

'I will?' The boy looked puzzled and uneasy suddenly; he glanced at Serenity who told him:

'Matt and I still have something we have to do,' his sister told him. For a minute Will's face seemed near grief.

Serenity had just found him, now she was going to leave him here in this strange place? He wanted to go home! Was everyone in his world always going to just ride off and leave him alone?

'It'll be fine,' Laura told him. She sat beside Will and put her arm over his shoulders. 'And it's just for a little while.' It seemed to comfort Will only a little.

'Just a short time,' Matt Holiday chipped in, placing his own bowl aside. He told Serenity, 'Speaking of which, we ought to have a talk about what we intend to do.'

'I think it is better if we talk along the trail,' Serenity said. Which might have meant she wanted to spare Will more worry or that she hadn't had time to think about a plan yet. Matt only nodded. He was trail-weary and now had a full stomach, and it was time to get some sleep. He rose and put on his hat.

'I thank you for the meal, Laura,' he

said. 'I think it's time Will and I hit the sack.'

'Yes,' Will said, also rising. 'I thank you for the meal.' Then astonishingly he went to Laura Kennedy and hugged her tightly. 'Goodnight.'

Serenity noticed the gesture and smiled. 'A full stomach and a man is forever grateful,' she said.

The night settled slowly. As Matt lay back to sleep in his bed, Will in the other, he listened to the night sounds of the Camelback saloons. He knew they would not cease entirely until close to morning. Men seldom quit drinking in a place like this until their money ran out or they were forcefully ejected. And it took some doing to get yourself tossed out of a Camelback saloon for your behavior. Sometime around three in the morning, Matt heard a group of riders heading almost silently out of town. Men 'off to work' without doubt.

Some of them would live to make their return.

The low piercing light through the

flimsy curtains of the room woke Matt not long after dawn.

Will was still sound asleep, a blanket drawn up over his head. Holiday went to the wash counter and peered at himself in the smoky mirror. His face showed few signs of his beating although his jaw still appeared slightly swollen. He had a razor in his bags and took the time to scrape the whiskers from his face. Satisfied with the result, he rinsed off and dressed. He was seated on the bed, stamping into his boots when there was a tap at the door. On opening it he found Serenity with a tray of food.

'Fresh bread and hot sausages,' she announced. She looked very sleek this morning in new twill trousers and a dark-blue blouse which must have belonged to Laura. Her hair had been polished to a luster and was then swept back and tied at the nape of her neck. Matt wondered if Serenity knew how beautifully she was put together. Probably so, he didn't believe women who said they didn't know they were pretty. Not those who owned mirrors, at least. These usually made small self-deprecatory remarks like, 'I think my nose is too big,' or some such other nonsense. They knew.

Will awoke sleepily as Serenity entered, crossed to the table and placed the platter down. She told them: 'The cook is really busy; this was all I could talk out of him. Besides,' she added to Matt, 'you don't even have to stop to eat. You can manage this along the trail.'

'Are we in a hurry?' he asked, strapping his gun-belt on.

'Well, we don't know, do we?' Serenity answered. The smell of fresh pork sausage and yeasty bread had hastened Will from his bed. She said to him:

'Now, when we leave, I want you to go to Laura's room, and stay there, do you understand? We'll be back as soon as we can.'

'All right,' Will grumbled. He was

folding sausage into a slice of thickly cut bread. Matt wondered if the boy was thinking of what had happened to Laura. What if they did not come back for him? Was he doomed to spend his life trapped in this outlaw town as well? Serenity seemed unaware of his feelings.

'Grab what you can carry, Matt,' she told him. 'We've got some miles to cover.'

By the time they had reached the bridge it was nearly full daylight. Serenity leaned forward in the saddle, her eyes intent. She had given up all pretense of only wanting to save Will from the outlaws. The thought of gold lit her dark eyes from within.

Pausing at the fork in the high road, Matt asked, 'Look here, Serenity, what is it you have in mind?'

'We need to keep an eye on Pete and the rest of them. They may have found the treasure trove.'

'It seems unlikely, the way they were going about it. I think they'll stand by their plan and wait for Frank Waverly to make an appearance. They may have lost their leverage — after all, they know by now that Will has gotten away — but your father can't be expected to know that they haven't got him still.'

'But we don't even know whether Father's coming — he still has months to go on his sentence,' Serenity said, the implication being that she was not going to wait months for her share of the money. 'We have to find it now.'

Matt sighed, his breath hissing through his teeth. 'Serenity, *I* have to find it, not you. If you have forgotten, that is my job and not yours. If you touch that money, you're liable to find yourself in prison as well.'

'You said they couldn't hold a new trial.' Her eyes danced and sparkled, the breeze shifted her raven hair. 'That the case was all settled.'

'That's not what I said at all. I said no one from the gang could be tried again for the same crime. They've served their time and legally they're free to go about their business, whatever that may be. You, on the other hand, have not been tried, convicted or served time for that robbery. If you still have an idea of running off with the money, you'd better forget it. I'm no lawyer, no judge, but you'll be guilty of some crime. What, I don't know: possessing stolen goods, theft of Butterfield property. I'm sure they'll find the correct term for it and certain that Butterfield will prosecute. They still want their money back.'

'But you . . . ?' Her eyes became vague, her lower lip trembled just a little. 'You wouldn't turn me in, would you, Matt? Anyway, what do you care what happens to the money?'

'It's a job I've taken on, finding that gold, and I mean to do my best at it,' Matt told her, but it seemed not to sink in. 'You could ride back to Camelback, collect Will and ride home,' he said. 'Your mother would be thrilled with that.'

'And we'll still be as poor as mice.'

'A lot of people go through their whole lives being poor, Serenity. You — you're just starting in life. You don't want to get off on the wrong foot.'

'Like a thief? An outlaw?' she snapped. 'What else would you expect of Frank Waverly's daughter? The only money we ever had, the only times we were happy, could afford to buy a few nice things, was when my father came back from a job with his saddle-bags bulging. We just became poor when he was caught.'

There was little logic in her words, but Matt thought he could see her point if he stood in her frame of reference. An outlaw always had the hope of a big payday; the less bold and more moral dirt farmer had none.

It didn't matter at the moment. They had not found the stolen gold; there was nothing to argue about. Matt did know that she would fight tooth and nail to keep it if they did. Her brief attempt at coquettishness had dissipated as if blown away by the cold wind which buffeted the side of the hill where they sat their horses. From there, in the new daylight, Matt could see how the place had gotten its name. A row of dun-colored hills rose to the west and another, similar hump rose to the east where they now sat. The place below could resemble a camel's back with some imagination.

Without a word, Serenity turned her roan up toward the hidden valley where the robbers' cabin rested. Matt followed, not knowing what else to do.

They had nearly topped out the rise, riding between stacks of massive yellow boulders, when Matt picked out a dark silhouette through the stands of manzanita screening the bend in the road. He grabbed the bridle of Serenity's horse and halted her. She turned fiery eyes on him.

'What now?'

Matt pointed ahead and mouthed the words, 'Someone's coming.' Who could it be but members of the Waverly gang? Why were they riding down from the valley now? Matt thought he knew. The one option for the gang that he had not considered before was that they would attempt to recapture Will Waverly. They would think first of Camelback, where they were undoubtedly welcome and where his rescuers would have to stop to obtain another horse.

Matt silently cursed himself. The boy had only Laura Kennedy to watch out for him, and he knew that Deke would have no compunction about telling the gang where the boy was. Matt yanked the head of Serenity's horse aside and led it into a wedge-shaped space between the head-high boulders. There was barely enough room to allow the two horses to enter the cleft. The clopping of the approaching horses' hoofs was loud in the stillness of the morning.

Serenity already had her Henry repeater out of its scabbard. The woman did tend to be quick with it, Matt had noticed.

The approaching hoofs drew nearer. Matt swung down from his buckskin and slipped behind one of the large fallen boulders. He had his Colt in his hand, but he was hoping the outlaws would not notice them in the niche and would pass by without a fight. After all, there was no point in gunplay at this time.

The first rider came into view, a grim-faced man wearing a long leather coat, riding a stubby bay horse. Matt withdrew farther into the pile of rocks. But he watched unbelievingly as the second rider passed and Serenity set the sights of her Henry rifle at him. Kneeling beside her horse, she took aim and before Matt could stop her, she triggered off.

The bellow of the .44–40 echoed through the close confines of their hiding-place. Matt watched one of the outlaws tumble from his saddle, saw the man riding behind him go to the side of his horse and fire beneath the neck of the animal. Bullets flew among the rocks, ricocheting wildly. Fragments of lead sang past Matt's head as Serenity's rifle spoke again. The last man in line whirled his mount and started back along the trail toward the valley above while the two remaining outlaws spurred their horses furiously down the hillside. Serenity was on her feet now. Her horse had shied and backed away. She ran forward, her rifle held at waist level, her eyes searching for further targets.

Serenity was panting as she stood over the body of the downed man. 'That'll teach them!' she said exultantly. Her eyes were bright with triumphal fire.

Teach them *what?* Matt was wondering as he turned over the outlaw and showed Serenity his dusty face. 'Do you know him?' he asked her.

'That's John Quirt,' Serenity answered. Her eyes had barely flickered toward the dead man's face. She was still watching for other targets, but there was none to be seen. The only thing moving along the trail was the dust from the bandits' fleeing horses. 'He was one of them,' Serenity said at length, lowering her rifle. 'Look in his saddle-bags, Matt. See if you find any gold.'

Reluctantly Holiday did, moving to the nervous, trembling bay the man had been riding. There was nothing in the saddle-bags but laundry, a box of .44 caliber ammunition, a skinning knife and a slab of beef jerky. He had been traveling light.

'Nothing here,' Matt told her, strapping the bags shut again.

'Then they haven't found it,' Serenity said with satisfaction. She now faced him, the wind pressing her white blouse against her body, tangling her hair. 'I'm going to follow the one who went back toward the cabin.'

'Why?' Matt asked.

'Why? That's where we intended to go, isn't it? Now we know there's only one man up there.'

'And we know that there are two traveling in the opposite direction, probably with the intent of finding your brother to take him hostage again.'

'They can't know Will is down there,' Serenity said, stepping even nearer to Matt, her black eyes glowing.

'All logic would point to that,' Matt disagreed.

'Maybe they were just riding down for some supplies,' Serenity said. 'Matt, we have to go after the lone man. I'm pretty sure it was Pete. I've seen him a few times before. He wouldn't have a chance against the two of us.'

'I have no wish to track down Whiskey Pete. Manhunting is not my kind of work.'

'Finding the gold is!'

Matt shook his head, thinking. Here he was, hired to find the lost payroll while Serenity had claimed that she was only interested in finding her brother. Their priorities had switched. Matt could not let the boy be taken again.

'I'm going down to make sure Will is safe. It'd be best if you came along with me, don't you think?'

But her eyes had hardened and shifted again to the upland trail. Did she now place the gold ahead of even her own brother's safety? Will wouldn't be hard for the outlaws to find. They would go to Deke's place first and ask. Deke had no motivation to protect the boy, no matter that he was Frank Waverly's son. Deke seemed to be a man who lived for the day, not one who would risk alienating the criminal gang. And what could Laura do to protect Will? What could she do to save herself?

He followed Serenity back into the niche to collect his horse. She swung aboard her roan lithely, shoving the rifle into its boot. 'Well?' she asked. 'Which way are you going, Matt?'

'I have to go back to Camelback. I'm needed there.'

'I knew I should never have hooked up with you!' she said in a brittle voice. 'Aren't you forgetting your obligation?'

She meant recovering the gold, but he wasn't so sure that her way of going about it was smart. Besides, Butterfield would pay him for this month's work no matter what, and if they decided to fire him, that was all well and good too. There were other jobs, other places to ride.

'I think one of us is forgetting,' Matt said, swinging a leg over the back of the buckskin. Then he rode it forward and turned down the long trail toward Camelback, a town he despised but did not seem to be able to get away from. His thoughts were on Will, now caught up in the backwash of his father's misdeeds, facing harm through no fault of his own.

And on the red-haired Laura Kennedy, who had had much of her life wasted by circumstances as well. Each of them deserved a second chance at living, and that hidden gold had nothing at all to do with it. Matt turned his back on the lost treasure and returned to the madness of the outlaw town alone.

7

It didn't take long for trouble to find Matt. He rode his horse to the Camelback stable, where he had had little luck. Slipping inside, he called out, but no one answered. There was someone there, though; a man he had not expected, but should have.

With his thoughts racing ahead to finding Laura and rescuing Will once more from the outlaws, he met this bump in the road with anger. As Davey Gillette stepped toward him, swaggering, a match-stick in his lips, Matt said coldly:

'I don't have time for this, Gillette.'

'Don't you? I have plenty of time, Waco — that's your name, isn't it? That's what people are saying.'

'I told you — '

'Told me that you don't have time for me. You had time to beat me up last night when I was doing nothing to you. Well, I was drunk last night, Waco. Now I'm sober.'

'It's not much of a pleasure to meet you either way,' Matt grumbled. 'Listen, friend, another time, another place. Right now I've got things to do.'

'So have I,' Gillette said, 'like teaching you a lesson. I've got a lot of friends in this town and I won't be humiliated in front of them.'

'None of them saw what you were doing, trying to attack Laura Kennedy.'

'None of them would care!' Gillette snapped. He stood before Matt in a bow-legged, balanced stance, his hand near his gun. 'What's the difference to you? Laura ain't much.'

'Be careful what you say, Gillette,' Matt warned him.

'Why? Because Ben Kennedy used to be a big man around here? He's dead now! Nothing about him troubles me. I'm tired of the brats coming here, thinking that we owe them some sort of special favors because their fathers slung a pistol. Like that woman you dragged in with. Who's she? Frank Waverly's daughter? Who cares about Frank Waverly any more, except for a few old-timers? Waverly's likely an old man now, anyway, locked up, dried out or dying. Who cares about those old-time gunnies?'

'You should,' Matt said in an even voice. Gillette eyed him up and down and smiled crookedly.

'You don't look like that much to me, Waco. Why are you standing for these women?'

'That's the way it's done,' Matt said, dropping the reins to his buckskin to free his hand. 'As you say, I might not be much, not a quick-draw artist or hard-bitten killer. But I've got more sand in my craw than a petty little woman-molester like you will ever have.'

Gillette seemed to puff up. His eyes swept the stable as if expecting help. Matt had wondered about that as well. Had he brought his friends with him?

Or did he have no friends willing to put their lives on the line for the sake of his dubious reputation?

Gillette had worked himself up into a fever of vengeful pride. 'Draw then, you bastard, and I'll see you in hell!'

To give him his due, Davey Gillette was quick with his gun, but he was none too accurate. The pistol in Gillette's hand exploded with fire and smoke and the sound racketed through the stable, panicking the horses. The bullet thudded into the wood of an upright post — very near to Matt's head, but missing by enough for his own shot, fired not so hastily, but more accurately, to tear into Gillette's chest near his heart. The outlaw was driven back by the force of the bullet, and he slapped at his chest wildly as if a hornet had stung him. He tried to fire again at Matt, but failed. His gun discharged into the stable floor, and it was over.

Matt glanced toward the stable doors, expecting a rush of men to come running to see what had happened. But it seemed that the populace of Camel-back did not get excited about a few shots being fired unless they were personally involved. None of Gillette's many so-called friends were drawn toward the brief commotion. It was no more than they heard every hour in one of the town's saloons.

Briefly Matt thought about reporting the shooting, but he had forgotten for those few seconds where he was. Shootings weren't reported in Camel-back; there was no one to report them to. He found that he was shaking as he holstered his Colt and led his buckskin to the water trough.

Well, he thought, that was one man out of the way, though he had never reckoned on Davey Gillette returning in the first place. He would have thought that the man had been too drunk the night before to even remember the incident. If Gillette had let well enough alone he would now be standing at his familiar bar, bragging about his past and future. That was the trouble with would-be badmen, Matt believed. Trying to live up to their brags frequently left them lying dead in the dust.

He filled a nosebag with oats and slipped it over the buckskin's head. The saddle he left fitted to the horse. In a gesture of decency, he dragged Gillette out into the yard behind the stable, but he did not bury the man. He had neither the tools nor the inclination for the task.

Besides, time was short. He had to reach Laura and Will. Two of the old Waverly gang were in town, and he had to find Laura and the boy before they could recapture their hostage. Leaving his horse, he walked the main street, if it could be called that. Water still ran there from the recent rains, and the mud was thick underfoot. He was unchallenged as he made his way toward Deke's place. Men thronged the saloons and plankwalks. Here and there a fistfight had spilled out into the muddy road. Some of these drew cheering or goading crowds, others were simply ignored by Camelback's jaded residents.

In another week, when the roads were dry, Matt knew, the outlaws would leave this town and its pale amusements, riding to wherever they had decided the best opportunity for their depredations had opened up. No one actually resided in Camelback, with the exception of bar owners like Deke. Everyone else was simply passing through, fleeing the reach of justice for their last escapade or planning their next bit of work.

Deke's seemed oddly silent on this day. There was a string of horses tied in front. Matt could not clearly remember the horses the outlaws had been riding. He decided that the back stairs were again his best entry point, but, as he made his way there through the alley, he halted suddenly.

A scraping sound from above caused him to pause and look upward. He could clearly see a man with a shotgun standing on the landing leading to the upstairs corridor. It was difficult to make out his features, but he was a big man, very big. Thick through the chest, wide across the shoulders. Big Bill Braddock? He did not know, never having seen the man or his portrait on a wanted poster. He did fit the description Matt had heard of him.

Why was he posted there?

Matt withdrew, turned again toward the main street and made his way to the front door of Deke's saloon. The place was ominously silent. The dozen men standing along the bar turned watchful eyes on Matt, but none said a word, and none was familiar to him. A trio of faded women wearing dresses with low-cut necks and short skirts sat together at one corner table, not speaking. Matt walked toward the stairs at the back of the saloon, smelling in passing the frying of beef steaks from the kitchen stove. Deke himself met Matt at the foot of the stairs.

'I wouldn't go up there, Waco,' the little man warned.

'Laura?' Was she in trouble?

'It's just a bad place to be right now,' Deke said, his eyes shifting away. Then he slipped past Matt and made his way to the saloon where he was greeted by a few of his regular customers.

Matt did not hesitate. Deke's warning meant nothing to him. He had to go upstairs and see what might have happened to Will and Laura, had to get them away from here somehow. His thoughts of Serenity and the lost gold were only distant and his concern for them faint. Serenity had decided to pursue her own way, dangerous though it might prove. Matt wasn't sure that he didn't pity the lone outlaw who had returned to the cabin.

All of that was only peripheral to his thinking. He concentrated on the shy, wide-eyed boy and on Laura, a prisoner within her own life, who now had capture or worse descending on them. For the men who had traveled as far and planned so long to recover the stolen Butterfield gold were not about to quit their quest just because of the small stumbling-blocks a young boy and a woman presented.

Something was up in Deke's place, that was for sure. The saloon was just too subdued. As Matt mounted the stairs toward the second floor where Laura's room was the silence was so profound to be almost palpable. Matt could hear the whispering of the wind beyond the walls of the building, nothing more. He slicked his Colt out of its holster and proceeded a step at a time, placing his boots next to the risers to limit any squeaks.

He mounted the last steps and stood at the end of the carpeted corridor, looking toward Laura's room. Still nothing moved. The other girls who had rooms up here were gathered in silence down in the saloon. Something had chased them downstairs, but what?

The man stepped out of the shadows of the landing alcove and leveled his pistol at Matt. 'Who the hell are you?' he demanded and started to draw back the hammer of his revolver. They were no more than ten feet apart. Matt fired his Colt. His bullet struck the stranger on his wrist. The heavy .44 slug nearly severed the hand. The shot, in the close confines of the hallway, was deafening; black smoke filled the corridor.

The gunman, his hand badly shattered, nevertheless shifted his pistol to his other hand and tried to get off a second shot at Matt. From the corner of his eye Matt saw a hall door open and a tall, shadowed figure appeared there. The shadowy man fired in his direction and Matt saw the man he was facing throw up his arms and collapse to the carpet, his pistol falling free.

Simultaneously the outer door to the landing opened and the big man carrying the shotgun burst in. Matt yelled out:

'Behind you!' and the man in the door to the room swung his pistol that way. He dropped to his knee and fired as the thunder of the twelve-gauge answered, spraying the walls with buckshot. Now black rolling smoke filled the corridor. Matt went forward cautiously but intently toward Laura's room.

'They're gone,' the stranger told him as he thumbed fresh cartridges into his pistol's cylinder. 'I sent them both away when I saw what these two had in mind.'

'Who are they?' Matt asked. He nodded toward the big man with the shotgun now lying inert in his fingers. 'I take it that was Bill Braddock.'

'It was. The other one,' the man said holstering his pistol, 'is Carl Hadley. Heard of them?'

'I have,' Matt answered. 'And you are . . . ?'

He already knew the answer. The tall man with the thin mustache smiled with a touch of sorrow, and replied, 'I'm Frank Waverly.'

He was of course, had to be. Who else would find Laura and Will, get them out of the room and stand to wait for their armed, would-be abductors?

'Where are they now?' Matt asked, entering the room which still held the lingering scent of that lilac soap that Laura used.

'Got her and Will a buggy and sent them south along the river road,' Frank Waverly said, seating himself on the bed. His gaze was intelligent, open. He did not appear to be a man on the run.

'South?'

'Heading back toward my old place. Will belongs home with Bertha — that's my wife — and the girl said she'd go along. Is she old Ben Kennedy's girl?' At Matt's nod, Waverly said, 'I thought so. That's one less debt I owe. Ben, he left the girl here when we went riding on a job that didn't go well. He got killed down in Alamosa.' Waverly's eyes narrowed. 'You seem to know a lot about everything that's going on here, but you don't look familiar to me. Who are you?'

'My name's Matt Holiday. I rode up here with your daughter, looking for Will. Braddock, Hadley, John Quirt and

Whiskey Pete were holding the boy hostage up at your old hideout. We got him out of there and brought him to Camelback.'

'So there's still two of them to deal with?' Waverly said, to himself more than to Matt. His eyes were on the window through which a patch of pale sky could be seen and the range of hills to the east, where the outlaws' cabin stood.

'There's only Whiskey Pete,' Matt told him. 'Serenity shot John Quirt dead on the trail.' Waverly looked briefly proud. Matt added, 'From ambush.'

'I don't get this,' Waverly said, standing. From down the hallway they could hear men carefully emerging to survey the damage. 'Where is Serenity now? You said you were coming to protect Will.'

'She decided to go after Whiskey Pete . . . and the gold.'

Waverly nodded heavily. 'You do know a lot about matters, don't you, Mr Matt Holiday?'

'Most of it,' Matt acknowledged. He said nothing about his own job, not knowing how far he could trust a man like Waverly. But then Waverly himself had come to Camelback to search for his son and had not gone chasing after the gold. Perhaps that was because he was the only man who knew where the treasure was hidden and felt no need to hurry.

Matt paused for a moment as Deke's head poked in to study him and Frank Waverly. The bar owner said, 'I knew you'd take 'em, Frank.'

'Thanks for your help,' Frank said and there was ambiguity in his tone.

'Sure, Frank. Anything else you need?'

'Nothing now.' He turned to Matt and said, 'Let's get going, Matt.'

'Go? Where?'

'After Serenity, where else?'

'Frank, I wanted to ask you . . . ' Matt began but Waverly cut him off with a gesture.

'We can talk along the trail. I'll tell

you anything you want to know.'

They started back into the hills, Frank Waverly on his palomino horse distinguished by an unusual black mark on its right jowl, Matt on his accustomed buckskin. The wind had freshened; the trail had become much drier. They spoke little at first. Halting their horses at the fork which divided the road to Camelback from the high country trail to the valley above, they looked down their back trail as the horses blew and the day turned itself toward evening.

'They're back there, you know,' Matt said. For he had seen three or four horsemen trailing after them.

'I saw them,' Frank Waverly said. 'I figured on it. There's men down there who are well aware of what would bring me back this way. The thought of gold is infectious.'

'Do you know who they are?' Matt asked.

'I can't make them or their horses out,' Frank said, squinting into the late sun down the road to Camelback, 'but my bet would be on Coyote Sam, Lou Walker and whoever else is riding with them these days.'

'I thought Sam was a friend of yours,' Matt said. Frank Waverly's mouth twisted into a wry smile.

'An outlaw only has two kinds of friends, Matt. The kind who are afraid of him and the kind who stand to make a dollar from him. Of course they would protect Serenity, but not out of friendship. They knew what would have happened to them if they let harm come to my girl. There can't be a man in Camelback who doesn't know that I have twenty thousand gold dollars stashed up here. That doesn't take away the caution they might feel about bracing me, but the thought of that much gold can fill a man with as much temporary courage as a pint of whiskey.'

Matt just nodded. If he had not always been completely straight in his dealings with his fellow man, he was at least happy to say he had never been an outlaw, forced to dwell in an outlaw's world.

They started up the steep trail toward the valley, speaking little. The mere effort was enough to inhibit conversation. They found the stubby bay horse John Quirt had been riding, still standing patiently at the entrance to the niche between the stacks of yellow boulders, nibbling at the chic plants that grew there, and they pulled up. Matt swung down to strip the saddle from the animal and slip its bit.

'Is Quirt still in there?' Frank Waverly asked, lifting his chin toward the niche.

'He must be. Think we should throw him over his pony's back?'

'I don't think so,' Frank said. 'We can't do a thing for him. No one down below would feel eager to bury him. Just do what you can for the horse — send it down the trail.'

The horse released, they started on their way and soon emerged on the grassy floor of the long valley. The cabin could not be seen, and there was no telltale smoke rising. Both men knew that there was at least one rifle waiting for them, though. It was up to Whiskey Pete whether he went to shooting or not. Matt thought he would now wait for Frank and hope for a cut of the stolen payroll.

What Serenity was up to was anyone's guess.

8

'They came to visit me one morning,' Frank Waverly was saying. They now rode the edge of the valley, again intending to reach the concealing pine trees on the wooded slope above the cabin. 'The warden and a man down from El Paso named Petty.'

Matt nodded. Warren Petty was a superior of his, though he did not tell Frank Waverly that. Waverly's intentions were still not clear. Both men were after the gold now, but after it was recovered, anything could happen, especially with Coyote Sam and his partners on their backtrail. Perhaps Frank felt they needed each other for the time being, but there was no telling how long that feeling would last once the gold was retrieved from its hiding-place, wherever that might be. For the moment Matt Holiday needed Frank Waverly even more than the bandit needed him.

Waverly went on as they neared the pine forest:

'I had five months left on my sentence, Matt. The warden said that he would let me out early with one stipulation.'

'That you bring the gold back,' Matt said.

'Of course. Otherwise, they knew they had almost no chance of ever retrieving it.'

'Must have been quite a decision for you.'

Frank Waverly shook his head and let his eyes focus on the forest ahead. 'No, really it wasn't. It wasn't just that I wanted out soon. I'd done four and half years. If need be I could do a few more months. It's just that all that time left me with hours, days to think things over, Matt. To think about what I'd done to Will, to Serenity and Bertha.

'I came to the realization finally that anything you take for free does nothing in the end but snatch freedom away from you — and I don't mean just being in jail. There's the freedom to ride where you want without having to look over your shoulder constantly, the freedom to enjoy wife and family without worrying when the law was going to arrive at your door . . . I don't know. I guess you could just say I decided to go straight, to give up the outlaw trail with all of its false promises of easy money.'

'Didn't they want to send someone along with you?' Matt asked.

'Oh, of course they did! I said I wouldn't do it that way — it could only lead to a pitched battle. I knew Pete and the boys had been released earlier, and I knew exactly where they would head. If it was only me riding in, they would try to relieve me of the gold. If I arrived with a couple of deputy marshals, they would start shooting the moment they spotted us.

'And,' Waverly continued, returning his gaze to Matt. 'this man Petty told the warden that they already had one of their men up here. That would be you, I guess?'

With some reluctance, Matt admitted, 'That's me.'

'I thought so,' Waverly said with a nod. 'How did you find them in the first place?'

Briefly Matt Holiday told the outlaw what had happened, how it had come about that he had ridden up here with Serenity.

'She doesn't know who you are?' Frank Waverly asked with surprise.

'Oh, she knows. I think she just figured she would need some help in this work. I was already headed this way to find Will, though I knew nothing about the cabin.'

'Careful!' Waverly said suddenly. 'We'd better get into the timber. I saw sunlight reflecting off something. It might have been a rifle barrel.'

'Would Whiskey Pete shoot at you?' Matt asked.

'I don't know what Pete might be thinking. Maybe that he can still negotiate a cut of the loot. He must believe that's due to him. The trouble is — now I can't make any sort of deal. I have to return the full amount, don't I?'

'Or go over me,' Matt told him.

How much of what Waverly was saying could be believed, Matt did not know. The man sounded sincere, but he could have invented the entire story. He did know Warren Petty's name, so a part of what he was saying rang true. But that was no guarantee that he meant to live up to his word, even if what he was saying was the truth. Frank Waverly had made a career of living outside the law.

At any rate, as a matter of caution, as they entered the forest once more, Matt slowed his horse a little, remaining behind Frank as he led the way through the pines.

Before they could reach the rise behind the outlaws' cabin, the purple shutters of evening had begun to close. The far hills were covered with shadows, the earth beneath the pines was a dark carpet. They paused and sat their winded horses on the overlook, studying the cabin below. No smoke rose from the iron chimney.

'Pete doesn't seem to be home,' Matt commented.

'He's down there. Where else would he be at this time of day?'

Frank Waverly's face was in sharp profile against the purple sky. His jaw was set, his teeth clamped. He had waited long for this moment and now seemed uncertain how to approach his objective.

'Where is she?' Waverly asked tightly. 'We can't make a move until we find Serenity.' No, they couldn't. Even if they found the gold, avoiding the watching eyes of Whiskey Pete and those of the men riding behind them, they could not ride off and leave Serenity to her fate. She had to be found.

'Do you think she's in the cabin?' Waverly asked.

'There's no telling. If so, where's

Pete? I can't see them making peace.'

'Neither can I,' Waverly said. 'Is she equipped to camp out?' he asked, for the night was already growing cool.

'No,' Matt told him.

'Then she'll either have to come to the cabin or head back toward Camelback.'

'She can't go back to town, not now,' Matt said, for he had been looking back across the night-shadowed valley. By the faint glow in the western sky and the light of a few feebly sparkling stars, he could clearly see the four men who were crossing the grassland riding toward them.

'Wonder who they are?' Matt said.

'I thought I told you. It's not much of a mystery to me,' Waverly answered. 'It has to be Coyote Sam, Lou Walker and a couple of their friends. Maybe those boys aren't too bright, but they saw Braddock and Hadley in town. Everyone in Camelback knows that they were with me when we got arrested for the Butterfield job. Braddock had to have come back for a reason. And they knew that Serenity was here as well, that she'd come riding out this way already.

'Then I showed up early this morning. Anyone could figure that we had come here because of the gold.'

'That's so,' Matt admitted. 'I guess it's a wonder that there aren't more of them.'

'I know Coyote Sam; he wouldn't want to share that information with just anyone. It would make his split of the gold too small. Besides why would they need more men? Four should be enough to take you, Matt, don't you think?'

'What about you?' Matt said, not liking the hint of threat in the cool gunman's words. If that was what it was.

'Me!' Frank Waverly laughed in the darkness. 'Why, no one is going to shoot me, Matt. No one. I'm the man with the key to the gold.'

'That's so, I guess,' Matt was forced to agree. 'Do you mind telling me now what you did with it?'

'Sure I mind,' Frank said flatly. 'I've made a deal with the authorities, remember? I have to be the one to return the gold.'

'You were sincere about that?' Matt asked.

'Yes, I was. I don't want them dogging me for the rest of my life. Matt, if you want a hint where the loot is, I'll give you this to ponder. It's by a tree!' He laughed again as Matt sat his horse in sullen silence. Now he lifted his eyes to the thousands, tens of thousands of pine trees that made up the surrounding forest.

'You're a humorous man, Frank Waverly,' Matt muttered.

'Not always,' Frank said soberly. 'For now, though, we've got to find some way of finding Serenity. Don't forget, they took little Will away to use as a bargaining tool. Someone might take it into his head to use Serenity for the same thing.'

'That's true, I'm afraid,' Matt agreed.

'We're going to have to look in the cabin, aren't we?'

'We are — before Coyote Jack and his crew get to it. Matt, let's give it a try. I'll go first. Whiskey Pete isn't going to shoot me for the same reason no one else will. I'm untouchable — until I have the gold. Then I guess, all bets are off.'

Approaching the cabin, Matt could hear the pines creaking in the wind, the clopping of their horses' hoofs. Nothing more. There was no sign of the incoming riders. Perhaps they actually did know nothing of the cabin, simply that Frank was said to have had some kind of hideout up here.

There was still neither sight nor sound of Whiskey Pete. They had to assume now that he was in the cabin, though they saw no horses. Frank supposed that he would have hidden his mount back among the trees.

And there was no sign of Serenity.

They knew the woman was up here, had to be. Where? As Matt had said earlier, he doubted that she and Pete had decided to throw in together. Serenity was a smart woman, smart enough to know that Pete might be tempted to hold her as a bargaining chip as he had done with her brother. Reaching the deeper shadows cast by the cabin, Frank Waverly swung down at the rear of the place and gestured for Matt to follow. Matt dismounted as well. The creak of leather seemed ominously loud in the still night.

Waverly already had his pistol in hand as he reached the corner of the cabin and started forward along the side which was windowless. Matt walked in his shadow, feeling uneasy, yet somewhat confident having Frank with him and only Pete, so far as they knew, to contend with.

The late moon still had not risen; the thousands of stars scattered against the cobalt-blue sky offered little illumination as they crept toward the front door of the cabin. Matt noticed light from a lantern, its wick turned low, behind the curtains, and the smell of smoke rising from the iron stovepipe was still present.

Frank had crossed in front of the closed door and now waited, half-crouched as Matt eased up to the other side. Waverly nodded and Matt rapped twice on the plank door to the cabin, using his gun butt. There was no response. Someone inside was trying to decide how to respond. Matt pulled his head back. It could be that the reply would be a barrage of bullets through the door.

Waverly cocked his head and pointed toward the door. Matt heard it too: the sound of footsteps cautiously approaching. He drew further aside and drew the cool curved hammer of his Colt back, cocking his pistol.

The light inside the cabin was dim, but it was almost overwhelmingly bright in their eyes as the door was flung open and they found themselves looking down the barrel of a big Henry repeater. Serenity squinted at them, lowered her rifle and said, 'Come on in, men.'

Frank entered first. His daughter threw her arms around him and looked up at his lined face. 'I was hoping you'd come, and soon, Father,' the dark-eyed girl said. Behind her a fire could be seen dimly flickering through the grate of the iron stove. It was warmer inside by far, and light enough to see by with the flickering lantern on the table. 'I was just hoping you'd get here,' she said.

'And Matt?' Frank asked drily.

'Matt!' the girl smiled. 'I knew he would come after me — sooner or later.'

For a moment she studied Matt Holiday, and he found himself hoping that she was not going to hug him as well. She did not. Serenity took Frank's hand and tugged him farther into the room after closing the door. Matt holstered his pistol and looked around the cabin interior.

'Where's Pete?' he asked.

'Where would you guess?' Serenity asked with a teasing smile. 'I got behind him and made him drop his guns. He's down there right now.' She nodded toward the cellar which had its trapdoor blocked once more by the weight of the heavy iron stove pushed over it.

'You didn't go back to Camelback,' Frank Waverly said, seating himself on a chair with cracked leather covering. 'Why not?'

Serenity perched on the chair's arm, her rifle still in her hands, and said:

'What would the point in that have been? Matt and I split up so that he could go and help Will, and I rode ahead to the cabin. It all worked out, didn't it?' she asked, indirectly revealing little concern for her young brother.

'Only because Frank showed up,' Matt said. Sullenly he walked to the table, pulled out a wooden chair and seated himself.

Still showing little concern about Will, she asked, 'Did you get them,

Father? Bill Braddock and Carl Hadley?'

'They won't be coming back,' Frank Waverly said. The eyes he fastened on his daughter now seemed disapproving, wary. Although Serenity did not ask, Frank told her, 'I sent Will and Laura Kennedy home along the river road. The river's fallen enough now for them to make it all right.'

'Laura?' Serenity asked with a sort of choked laugh. 'Why is she involved in family business all of a sudden?'

'She has been for a while,' Matt reminded her.

Frank Waverly said, 'I didn't want the boy trying to drive a team that far alone. Matt had to come back here; Laura wanted to go.'

'She's up to something,' Serenity said, rising to face both her father and Matt Holiday. 'I know it. Her father was — '

'A crook like me?' Frank asked. 'Ben Kennedy was an outlaw, but he was straight with his friends. His daughter wouldn't have ended up stuck in Camelback if not for me. I'm the one who led Ben into that shoot-out. I owed him; I owe her.'

'Oh, all right then,' Serenity said petulantly. Frank's eyes flickered and the beginnings of a grimace pulled at the corners of his mouth. Perhaps, Matt thought, Serenity would never have dared to talk to her father like that when he last saw her.

Four and a half long years ago.

'At any rate,' Serenity went on, walking to the dead fireplace where she rested an arm along the mantel, 'we're in the clear now. No one's chasing us; the gang's broken up. We can just sack the money and head home.'

'Not exactly,' Matt said. 'There's some men chasing us who have other ideas.'

'It looks like Coyote Jack and his friends have a notion of grabbing the gold,' Frank said. Serenity's eyes narrowed.

'All we have to do is lay an ambush

— they can't possibly take it by main force,' Serenity believed. Her eyes had narrowed, emphasizing her catlike appearance. They caught the glint of the light from the stove. Matt glanced at Frank Waverly, trying to gauge his mood. He had begun to like the man; he hoped that ambush was not what Frank had in mind.

'There's more to it,' Waverly told his daughter. 'I have to take that money back or return to prison.' Serenity seemed unconcerned.

'With twenty thousand we can run far enough for no one to be able to follow us,' she said. 'Even if they did catch you, it would only be another five or six months, isn't that right?' She seemed unconcerned about her father returning to prison.

'It's not only that,' Frank told her. 'I've decided that it's the only thing to do. I want to start over with a clean slate and a clear conscience.'

'What has happened to you!' Serenity erupted. 'Did they have a Bible in every cell of that prison? You fought for that money, served time for it. It's ours — yours, Father.'

'No,' Frank Waverly said heavily. 'It's not. It never was. It belongs to other men.'

Serenity only stared for a minute; her jaw had dropped a little in amazement. 'What did they do to you, Father, remove your heart down there? You know how much I . . . Mother and Will and I need something to live on. The money belongs as much to you as anyone else. Who talked you into this madness?' she asked.

Her eyes shifted to Matt Holiday's shadowed face. 'Was it this bounty hunter who's convinced you? Has he forced you into a bargain?'

Serenity's gaze indicated that she thought that Matt could be taken care of easily enough if he were responsible.

'Let's just say that I was convinced,' Frank Waverly said, rising. 'Serenity, you have to try to understand. I am doing this for you, for Mother and for

Will. I'll be gaining much more than I'll be losing. Maybe I'm just getting older, less reckless. I only want to live what they call a normal life. I am tired of days on the run, nights sleeping on the prairie, having every man who owns a gun waiting for a chance at me. Friendless, loveless, cold, hungry and alone.'

Serenity turned away, gnawing at her lower lip. Matt rose and said, 'We've got men on our backtrail. We'd better set up a plan for standing guard. Tomorrow is going to be no better than today was.'

9

Serenity had taken the last watch. Now the morning sun was cresting the pine-clad slope behind the rough cabin. Whatever warmth it would bring to the day was not apparent yet. The grassy meadow stretched out before the house glistened where the new sun caught the dew on it, making jewels of the water drops.

Serenity walked to the stove again and threw in the few remaining bits of cut wood. She yawned, placed her rifle aside and looked around the miserable room. Her father slept, his back to her, but Matt Holiday was awake, sitting up, his blanket around his shoulders. Serenity was impatient with their slow rising. She wanted to recover the stolen money and get out of there as soon as possible. Now that they knew there were hunting men on their backtrail, there was no time to waste.

'We have to get moving,' she said. Matt Holiday nodded.

'You're right.'

'I hate to wake Father,' Serenity said.

'I'm awake,' Frank Waverly grumbled beneath his blanket.

'We have to be on our way.' Serenity's voice was taut, but from subdued excitement, not from fear. To Matt it seemed that Serenity had no fear.

Beneath the floorboards they could hear insistent pounding. 'What do we do about Pete?' Matt asked.

'I don't know. Let him out, I suppose. What if none of those men behind us thinks of looking for him down there — or cares a thing about him?'

'You're right, I suppose,' Matt said. One more enemy to be dealt with.

'I've got his guns,' Serenity said as Frank rose and stepped into his boots. 'He won't give us any trouble.'

'Well, if that's what we have to do,' Matt said, 'let me give you a hand moving the stove.' He looked at Serenity's slender form and wondered how she had managed to shift the iron stove by herself. She was a strong and determined woman, no doubt about it.

It was easy work for the three of them and within minutes they had the stove off the trapdoor to the root cellar. Serenity, rifle in hand, and Matt stepped back from the trap while Frank Waverly swung it open.

'Climb up out of there, Pete,' Frank said.

'Frank? Is that you? Well, I'll be damned.'

They heard boot leather on the ladder rungs and then Whiskey Pete's head emerged from the cold darkness below. He was a short man with a trace of beard. His eyes were quietly menacing despite the little puckered smile he wore.

'That was hell. Worse than a prison cell,' he complained, moving close to the nearly dead stove for warmth. 'I about froze to death down there.'

156

'Imagine what it would have been like for a kid,' Matt Holiday said. Pete glanced at him but made no response.

'Well, anyway, I am sure glad to see you, Frank. How about you let me have my share of the money and I'll be on my way?'

'I haven't got it yet,' Frank told him. 'When I do, I'm sorry for you, Pete, but it's all going to be returned.'

'What are you talking about!' Pete had lost his fake smile. He glared at Waverly. 'I waited four years for my cut of the loot. Four hard years. And you can't say I didn't earn my share of it.'

Frank Waverly's voice was cold. 'You have a point, and I might have felt a little bad about cutting you out . . . if you hadn't snatched my boy. Grabbing Will cut you out of any consideration, Pete.'

'We didn't hurt him none,' Pete sniveled. Frank didn't accept that.

'You took him away from his mother, dragged him up here and threw him into the root cellar,' Waverly shot back.

157

'You did your prison time locked up for something you did do. Will did nothing at all to any of you.'

'You're not going to change your mind?' Pete asked, his eyes searching Frank's face.

'I'm not. Where's your horse?'

'Back in the trees.'

'Get on it and ride,' Frank said, his voice steely. 'That's the best deal I'll offer you.'

Pete was going to resume whining, cajoling, perhaps threatening, but he could see the resolve in Frank Waverly's eyes. He was getting nothing from the man.

'This is a hell of a way to treat an old partner,' Pete muttered. 'Let me have my guns.'

'No,' Serenity said firmly. Pete shifted his glare to her. 'You're liable to get ideas.'

'Well, damnit all!' Pete said, throwing up his hands in frustration. He wiped his wrist across his mouth, shrugged his shoulders and said, 'I guess I'll be going then.' He started toward the door, adjusting his hat. Reaching it, he turned and asked in a sorry tone of voice, 'Frank, could you let me have ten dollars? I'm riding back to Camelback, and I hate to go in naked.'

Before Frank could answer, Matt slipped a ten-dollar gold piece from the pocket of his jeans and flipped it toward Pete, who caught the bright spinning coin and nodded, putting it away. Going out, Pete left the door open to the cool of morning. Frank stood watching, pistol in hand.

'Wait until we see him ride away,' he told them. 'Pete's been known to carry an extra revolver in his saddle-bags.'

Either he wasn't on this occasion or thought better of trying to face down Frank Waverly, for after a few minutes they saw Whiskey emerge from the pines and ride down the slope toward the flats below. Once he turned his head and glared back at them; it was almost possible to read his thoughts. They weren't pretty.

'All right,' Frank said, snatching up his Stetson. 'Let's do what we came to do.'

Frank led the way on foot. Since the outlaw had not swung aboard his horse, Matt followed afoot as well, leading his buckskin horse. Serenity came last. When Matt glanced at her, her eyes were glitter-bright. The glow had nothing to do with the morning sunlight now filtering through the trees, spraying fans of light.

Frank halted and waited for them at the base of a twin pine tree. Around them jays squawked and gray squirrels chattered, bounding from branch to branch. Matt frowned as he approached Waverly. His eyes were on the ground, where there was no sign of digging, of the earth ever having been disturbed. Nor was there a blaze on the tree, or any sort of mark to indicate that it was special in any way.

'Are you sure, Father?' Serenity asked almost breathlessly. She held the reins to her roan horse which tossed its head in irritation or simply out of high spirits. 'Don't we need a shovel?'

'I can't see what for,' Frank answered, his eyes lightly amused. 'You're probably agile enough.'

Then he pointed upward into the lower branches of the tree where a pair of saddle-bags hung like strange leather fruit. 'That's what we are after,' Frank said.

Matt admired the man's instincts. Frank had had to do his work quickly to conceal the gold from the rest of the gang, and there had been no time to dig. But under the ground is where men naturally expect to find hidden treasure. That was the reason that the other day they had seen Pete, Braddock, John Quirt and Hadley comb the area without success. Riding with their eyes to the ground, none of them had bothered to look up.

While Matt stood pondering, Serenity had led her roan to the base of one of the pines, stepped up onto the saddle and grabbed onto the lowest hanging bough. She went up the tree like a cat and slipped the weathered saddle-bags from the branch.

'Step back,' Frank told Matt. 'There's about fifty pounds of metal coming down.'

The heavily laden bags hit the ground with a thud. Serenity landed softly on the ground a few seconds later and rushed to them, going down to her knees in the pine needles. She had the buckles on the bags opened before Matt even reached her. The saddle-bag leather was weathered, brittle and cracked, but its contents shone as brightly as on the day the coins were minted. Serenity remained on her knees for long minutes, admiring the treasure. Frank and Matt exchanged a glance, then looked away.

'I can see them coming,' Waverly said, pointing toward the west, across the grassland. 'We'd better get moving.'

Looking that way, Matt too saw the group of four men riding toward them. Only four. Where was Whiskey Pete, then? Perhaps he had decided after all to ride back to Camelback and find out how much whiskey ten dollars could buy for him there.

'Yes, let's get going,' Matt said. Waverly crouched and fingered the cracked leather of the saddle-bags.

'We can't use these,' he said. 'We'd better split it up into our own bags.' He glanced up to find Matt staring down at him.

'We'd better keep it all together,' Matt Holiday told him. 'My bags are new.'

'All right then,' Frank said, catching Matt's meaning. Serenity stood aside, her eyes gleaming as they transferred the gold into Matt's saddle-bags and tied them down behind the buckskin's saddle.

'What are you planning on doing next?' Frank asked as he knotted a piggin string over the saddle-bag strap.

'First we get off this mountain,' Matt said, 'then we take Serenity home. You and I can travel on to El Paso. We'll turn the gold into Warren Petty at the Butterfield office. He'll get a telegram off to the prison warden and you'll be as free as a bird.'

Frank continued to rest one hand on the saddle-bags. He smiled ruefully. 'That's the only way to go about it, isn't it?' he said at last, and Matt believed that Frank Waverly had given up any thought of keeping the gold. But El Paso was a long way off; he believed Frank was sincere, but wasn't going to make the mistake of trusting him utterly.

'We aren't going to stand and fight them, are we?' Serenity asked, now appearing anxious as the riders below neared.

'No,' her father told her, swinging aboard his neat little palomino pony. 'There's other ways out of here. The road you've used is just handiest because it leads to Camelback.'

Matt swung into his own saddle. The buckskin shuddered a little and side-stepped. It had carried more extra

164

weight than the fifty pounds of gold before, but that did not mean it had a liking for the added burden.

'Lead on,' Matt said to Frank, glancing behind him to see that Serenity had mounted her bad-tempered roan. In this situation Frank Waverly would have to take the lead, he was the only one who knew the trail out. Matt found himself wishing that he could find a way to manage riding behind Serenity as well. It was growing more difficult to trust the dark-haired beauty. She rode with her Henry rifle across the saddle bow, looking young, fresh and as attractive as ever.

There was no way of telling what was going on behind those shining black eyes.

They rode on, upward for a while, through the forest which was now mixed pine and cedar. Frank knew his way after years spent in this country. It was a good thing the outlaw rode with them, Matt considered. He himself would be lost, perhaps even tempted to try fighting his way past the men on the backtrail.

An hour later they had crested the shoulder of the mountain, and Frank reined his horse in to explain to the others. 'That's called the Killeen Cut-off,' he said, indicating a steep, winding, very narrow trail down the flank of the deep valley ahead. 'It's a good enough road if the rain hasn't washed a few tons of mud and rock down to block it.'

'If it has?' Serenity asked.

'If it has — we're stuck,' Frank Waverly said grimly.

'There's no other choice, is there?' Matt commented. 'Let's get going.'

As they rode lower down the flank of the mountain, the trees thinned and then were gone. Only an occasional lone pine stood on the slopes here. They reached the road which wound its way both up and down the flanks of the hills.

'That way,' Frank said, nodding toward the north. 'There used to be a silver mine. It never amounted to much and finally played out. It probably cost them more to grade this road than they took out of the mine, but the ore wagons had to have a way to get in and out.'

'I'll wager it wasn't of much use in the rainy season,' Matt said. When they reached the road it only confirmed his statement. The narrow trail was still deep with mud. Matt could see where the road had once been wider, wide enough for wagons to pass, but so much of the banks had sloughed off onto the road that it was only a treacherous-appearing ribbon wending its way down the slope-sided canyon toward the flats, far away.

'It's not as bad as it looks,' Frank told them. 'I haven't ridden it in years, but with any luck we'll make it all right.'

The wind gusted against them as they worked their way down along the faint trail, all that remained of the old mine road. At first the road was wide enough for them to have ridden side by side, but as they rounded a bend there was a wash-off in front of them where tons of mud and rocks had come loose from their grounding, and now a wide tongue of earth lay mounded across their way.

'We can't go over that!' Serenity said correctly. The only thing to do was skirt the washed-off debris. Looking downward Matt saw that the road here fell off steeply into the canyon below. It was something like 300 or 500 feet straight down and the bit of road they had left to follow along it was no more than three or four feet wide.

'I don't like this,' said Matt, who had a vague fear of heights.

'Want to go back?' Frank Waverly asked with a faint smile.

'No, I don't.'

'Come on then. It's not so bad if the rim of the road is firm enough.'

If it was not they would slide, man and rider into the rocky depths of the canyon. The wind gusted with unexpected fierceness as they started warily onward. Frank led the way. His little palomino picked its way delicately around the fallen material. The horse's mane and tail drifted wildly in the wind. It was no more than a hundred feet along the trail that they had to travel to reach the clear road again, but it seemed like miles as Matt urged his leery buckskin forward.

The buckskin did not have the mincing little steps that the palomino had. It plodded on, head up, eyes wide. Matt leaned to the inside of the trail, the wind buffeting him. Above, along the cliff face, he thought he heard a groaning. What if more of the mud and debris decided to slide down? He glanced only once toward the depths of the canyon. A man falling that way would have no chance, not a one, of surviving.

'Are you going on or not?' Serenity's voice demanded from behind him. She showed only impatience, wanting to get this over with. If Matt's horse stumbled and slid over taking him and the gold in his saddle-bags, she would not be in that mood. Matt walked the horse forward. At times it seemed that the buckskin was so near to the rim that its hoofs could not clear the way. Matt had slipped his boots in the stirrups back to their toes. He had decided that if the worst came to the worst, he would try to leap aside.

He did not have to. He was suddenly on wide, open road again. Frank Waverly was waiting there, a nervous grin on his face.

'You made work out of that,' the outlaw said as Matt reached him.

'I didn't like it, Frank. I didn't like it a bit,' Matt admitted. He removed his hat and wiped his brow. Despite the chill wind, he was perspiring freely.

'Are we going to sit here jawing?' Serenity asked sharply. Her face showed no concern. She might have been out on a Sunday ride.

Without answering, Frank led off down the trail. Rounding an inside bend, the road briefly widened out to its intended broadness, large enough for an ore wagon. The ground was much firmer underfoot, though the cliffside rising to the right of the trail was twice as high. It was composed of gray granite which must have been blasted away with dynamite; there was little loose material on it to have been washed free by the rain storm.

They passed through the niche in the stony hill and rode the trail downward. It had narrowed again, was slick, but nothing like it had been at the trailhead. Ahead now, Matt could see flat prairie. Once he thought he caught the glint of the river, but he might have been mistaken.

Now the hills rising on either side sprouted wind-twisted scrub juniper and the inevitable stands of nopal cactus. Among the rocks there was some new grass growing. Matt saw a group of very young cottontail rabbits munching at the silver-green foliage. They had water from the recent rain, new grass growing, the shelter of the boulders. It was a good time to be a rabbit. They were as of yet innocent of snakes, coyotes and men with guns.

Ahead in the road now, they saw where a scattering of boulders had fallen from the heights, blocking off the entire road. Frank turned in his saddle and said to Matt, 'It looks like we have a little work to do.' For though the rocks were not many, the horses could not clamber over them. The road would have to be cleared.

Matt swung down from the saddle and went with Frank to the line of boulders. Most were head-sized or smaller, a few the size of a house, but they believed they could clear enough of a path through them for the horses with a minimum of labor.

'I'd bet a lightning strike caused this,' Frank said, looking up at the barren rock face. 'I've seen it happen before.'

Matt did not waste time speculating. He got to work shifting the rocks, rolling them aside. It didn't take them long to clear a path through the fallen granite rocks, but long enough for Matt to start perspiring again, long enough for his shoulders to begin to ache. Frank, although the older man, worked steadily, without visible signs of soreness. Maybe his prison labor had kept him in good shape.

Matt stood up, stretching his back. The wind continued to grow, the temperature to drop. With a sigh he shifted his feet and reached down for one last rock. Three things happened at once: Frank Waverly slammed him to the ground with his shoulder, a gun shot rang out, the bullet clipping fragments from a boulder beside Matt's head.

And his buckskin horse, with its saddle-bags full of gold, went racing wildly past him toward the empty flats below.

10

When Matt turned his head to look up into the glare of the sun, he saw Frank Waverly standing over him with his gun drawn. He started to rise, but Frank motioned him back to the ground.

'I told you to keep your head down,' the outlaw hissed.

'What's this all about? Matt demanded.

'Someone took a shot at us from up on the ridge,' Frank said, indicating the tall granite bluff towering over them.

'How could anyone have found us?'

'I don't know. It's someone who knows about this trail. He followed us along the rim rock. But he's stuck now,' Frank said. 'There's no way he can cross the gorge.'

Slowly Matt sat up, his eyes on the canyon top and on Frank Waverly's gun. 'Did my horse run off when he shot?' Matt asked.

'He sure did,' Frank said with a wicked grin. 'Serenity took him.'

Matt muttered an inarticulate curse and sat up. 'What do we do now, Frank?'

'We're sort of pinned down at the moment, I'd say,' Waverly answered. 'I can't make out a target above us, but he's shown he can see us just fine. At a guess, I'd say he's trying to keep us here while the others ride down the road and catch up.'

'Do you think they can?'

'They weren't that far behind us.'

Matt got into a crouch and peered over the fallen rocks. 'Then I guess we'd better take our chances and make a run for it.'

'We'd better,' Frank agreed. He added, 'Besides, we have to catch up with Serenity. It'll be a little tough with only a single horse between us.'

'Frank,' Matt asked, 'do you think she just panicked when the gunshot sounded — or is she making her play for the gold?'

'How would I know?'

'You know her better than I do.'

'Do I?' Waverly replied. 'I haven't seen her for four and a half years. When I was home, I didn't show her anything but the swagger and boasting of an outlaw. I don't know who she is, Matt, or what she would do. If I had to guess . . . yes, I think she means to keep the gold.'

Matt was thoughtful for a moment. 'Losing that money puts the both of us in a bind.'

'Does it not?' Waverly said sourly. His eyes continued to search the cliff top, but he could find nowhere to put his sights. 'We'd better make our run for it before someone does come down the trail behind us.'

'Will your horse carry double?' Matt asked, eyeing the young palomino that Waverly rode.

'He'll have to, won't he?' Frank said. 'Come on, Matt. We've got trouble behind us, and more than a little ahead.'

Matt got quickly to his feet and followed Frank, moving as close to the wall of granite as possible to avoid giving the sniper a clear downward shot. No bullets followed them as they reached the palomino. Frank gathered up the reins and swung aboard. Gesturing, he took his boot from the left stirrup and held out his hand so that Matt could swing up behind him.

They started again down the narrow trail. Riding behind Waverly, Matt swiveled his head frequently, watching for the approach of their pursuers. Perhaps, seeing the state of the trail, they would give it up, but Matt did not think so. Gold worth $20,000 provides a lot of motivation.

It must have been an hour on, no more than two, when the trail fanned out and flattened as it met the level prairie. The wind was not so cold here, but still it gusted, flattening the grass, making a flag out of the little palomino's white tail.

'I don't see a sign of Serenity,' Matt said. 'Do you?'

'She wouldn't ride directly south,' Waverly believed. 'She'll head for the river and make her way downstream. She'll have water for the horses and the cover of the willow brush.' Matt nodded, knowing that Frank was telling him what he himself would do in similar circumstances.

'So we go after her?'

'I can't see us making up any ground on her by doing that,' Waverly answered. 'Not on one horse. The only trouble with following the river is that it meanders, forms a few oxbows. If we reach it a mile or so south, we might find ourselves ahead of Serenity.'

The man had obviously ridden some crooked trails in his time. An outlaw must always be thinking of the surest way to make his escape. Matt wondered how experienced the men following them were at making such determinations. They would know one thing for sure: even without knowing about

Serenity, Frank Waverly would be heading for his home. Frank glanced at him and Matt nodded.

The outlaw started the horse, lifting it to a steady trot which seemed quick enough, but not tiring to the small animal carrying double for the first time. Its hoofs sang through the silver green grass, at times starting quail and partridge from their feeding. After another long hour, they had come in sight of the river, its course marked by long ranks of willow brush and sycamore trees, taking their nourishment from the flow of its water.

Frank now slowed the horse a little and in minutes they were walking it through the brush and riverside trees. The silver glint of the river's face was sparkling in late sunlight. At the edge of the river both men slipped from the horse's back and let it lower its muzzle into the cooling stream.

'What do you think?' Matt asked.

'You mean do I think that we're ahead of her? If her plan was to follow the river, I think so,' Frank said. His eyes lifted to the far bank of the river. 'If she decided just to cross over and line out toward the west, we'll probably never see her again.'

Matt pondered that thought. 'I think she really is concerned about her mother,' he said at last. 'I think she'll try to make sure that Bertha gets some of the money to get along on.'

Frank nodded, saying nothing but obviously thinking of many things.

'Let's hope so,' Frank replied at last. 'I'm the one responsible, you know. I haven't had a cent to give Bertha in four and a half years. I always thought I'd be back with even more money, but that was just vanity and pride, wasn't it? It's been hard on Serenity too, I imagine. No new dress to wear, no bit of jewelry. Serenity is not my blood daughter, but just the same, I was her father, and I failed her as well. I was a selfish man, a bad father. Wouldn't you say so, Matt?'

'I'm not one to judge,' Matt Holiday

said. 'I do know that only a man with a heart is willing to look at himself and ask such questions. A villain does not.'

Frank made a sudden gesture for silence. 'Someone's coming,' he said through his teeth as he unsheathed his Winchester rifle from its saddle scabbard. It didn't seem possible, but the Camelback gang had caught up with them. Of course they had fresher horses and none were carrying double. Still it was a bit of a shock to see the riders emerge from the brush.

Matt recognized them all: Coyote Sam, Lou Walker, and the nameless bearded man from the stable . . . and riding last, leading the tethered palomino, the old gunman, Elias Foss.

Seeing Matt and Waverly they reined up sharply, and Frank headed for his horse while Matt bolted for the surrounding brush. He raced through a thick stand of willow brush, tore his shirt and arm on a thorny mesquite branch and then hunkered down in the insect-plagued thicket.

He hadn't expected Frank Waverly to run, but then what was the outlaw to do, draw down on four armed men?

They had his buckskin horse with them — what did that mean for Serenity? Had they stolen it, knocked her down and led it off, or . . . ?

Warm, sun-bright minutes passed in the thicket where Matt had taken cover. Sweat ran down his arm and dampened the hand holding his Colt revolver. Gnats swarmed around his head; something reptilian slithered past him. Wiping at his eyes with the back of his cuff, he rose to his feet, trying to peer through the screen of brush, trying to come up with some sort of plan. Where had Frank gotten to? He had not heard the sound of his horse racing away, heard no shots.

Matt knew he had to make a move. He was too close to success to give it up now. With painful slowness he circled through the heavy brush, trying to make his way behind the pursuing men. If they were still there, which seemed unlikely. Why should they choose that particular place to pause, especially knowing that Matt and Frank were near by? With no option, he continued on, working through the head-high brush toward the river. It seemed futile, but he did not know what else to try.

Through the willows now he could see the glinting of the river, hear a fish jumping, and then men's voices.

'Well, we knew they were out here somewhere.'

'Yeah, but now there's no need to track them. I say let them go. We've got what we came for.'

'I don't like having Waverly around us. There's no telling what he might do.'

'Let's just pull out, boys. Ride straight back to Camelback.'

'Then we're liable to have Frank and that Waco on our back trail!'

This last speaker was Coyote Sam, Matt knew. The outlaws were in disarray, that was clear. They had the gold, but what now? Returning to Camelback was unattractive for a number of reasons. For one, as they had noted, Matt and Frank Waverly would be forced to ride after them. Besides Camelback was not a good place to light for men with 20,000 gold dollars in their pockets. There were men there who would think nothing of stripping them clean.

'El Paso's good for me,' someone — Lou, Matt thought — said.

'That's a lot of open country to ride, especially with those two behind us,' Elias Foss, recognizable by his whiskey-cracked voice, put in.

'All right!' Lou snapped, 'Then just what is it you think we should do?'

Matt was at the verge of the brush now, he could see the men clearly. He himself had no plan; he certainly wasn't prepared for the voice that rang out from the river's edge.

'Why don't you just give it back?' Serenity shouted. 'Sneak up on me and steal that horse, would you!' Matt spotted her then, sitting her little red roan, her hair in a tangle, falling across her face, concealing her eyes. She had her Henry repeater to her shoulder, and as Matt spun that way she fired the rifle.

Lou Walker turned around, reached for his holstered gun, staggered toward the river and fell face forward into the water, his head bobbing in the current.

'You little wolf cub,' Coyote Sam yelled, taking cover behind his horse as Serenity fired again. The bullet hit the dun horse's flank and the animal danced away in pain, holding its right rear leg high. Sam fired back.

Serenity did not react, so apparently he had missed her, but her next shot was on target. As Matt watched, Sam backpedaled away, his white shirt stained with a crimson rose. His face was bloodless, his eyes utterly white as he threw up his hands and fell to the sand on the river's edge. Elias Foss had his rifle out, and he was ready to return fire, but a shot from behind him turned his sights.

Frank Waverly had returned. His

six-gun in his hand, he was calmly firing at the hijackers. Foss shouted out wildly, 'It's me, Frank! Elias Foss!'

And then he wasn't Elias Foss any more, he was nobody. He was only a crumpled heap of carrion on the river's shore. The last man, the bearded one with no name, had swung into the saddle and raced it toward the willow brush, not ten yards from where Matt waited. The thick-chested sorrel horse he rode broke into the brush like a rampaging bull. A few shots followed the rider, but died down when there was no target left on which to sight.

Matt rose from concealment to snag the sorrel's bridle with his left hand. The animal's head snapped back in annoyance, then the horse stopped short, sending its rider over its head to land in the thorny thicket. The bearded man hit the ground hard. Matt thought at first that he had broken his neck, but slowly he recovered, his breath coming in tight gasps. Matt was on him in seconds. He slipped the pistol from the outlaw's holster and winged it away, waiting for the man to catch his breath enough to sit up and wait, holding his head in his meaty hands.

'That's enough, friend,' Matt said.

'It is, isn't it?' the man with the beard agreed. He looked up mournfully, his dark eyes dull and pained. 'Let me go, Waco. There's no point in sending me to prison.'

'Maybe, maybe not,' Matt said coldly. 'That isn't what I had in mind. For trying to grab that gold you'd probably only get a few years. But,' he went on, 'in this country they still hang horse thieves.'

The man's eyes grew wide. His face paled. 'You wouldn't . . . it wasn't me that took it!'

'That buckskin is my horse, and I always favored it. I saw you with it.'

'There's not just me — the others took it too.'

'You're the only one that's left,' Matt said. 'I'd rather you didn't get out of prison some day and come looking for me. If we hang you, on the other hand — '

'Don't do it! I don't want to swing. There must be another way!' the man said miserably.

Matt appeared thoughtful. He nodded. 'If you go back to Camelback.'

'I will if you say so,' the bearded man said, getting to his feet as rapidly as his battered body would allow. 'I swear it!'

'Then get going,' Matt ordered.

'Sure, Waco. Sure. Thanks,' he said, reaching for his horse's reins.

'Just you,' Waco said, gesturing with his gun barrel. 'Not the horse. I can't take a chance on you coming after us.'

'I swear I won't! You can't do this, Waco. Do you know how long it would take me to walk to Camelback — if I could even make it?'

'It's a tough life,' Matt said. 'Get going or we manage things another way. With a rope.'

The man stroked his beard, wiped his sweaty face and moved off slowly through the riverside brush. Matt watched and waited for a few long minutes until he was sure the man was gone and then started back toward the river, leading the bearded man's sorrel. Frank Waverly and Serenity were waiting. So was Matt's buckskin horse.

'Did you take care of him?' Frank asked.

'I did,' Matt replied.

'We didn't hear a shot,' Serenity said, stepping toward him, her eyes suspicious and challenging. She gripped her rifle tightly.

'I didn't shoot him. I sent him walking back to Camelback.'

Waverly nodded his understanding, but Serenity was furious. 'You just sent him walking off! After what he, all of them, tried to do? What if he decides to come back?'

'Without a horse or a gun,' Matt told her. 'With the three of us here — I'd be more than a little surprised. Besides,' he said, 'that's not the sort of work I was sent up here to do.'

'You still intend to take the gold back

to Butterfield!' Serenity said in aston- ishment. 'After what it's cost us?'

'Yes. That's what I intend to do. It still doesn't belong to us. You can understand that, can't you?'

'No,' she snapped, 'maybe I can't!' She stalked away toward her waiting red roan and swung into the saddle. Matt looked to Frank for help. 'Maybe you can explain to her how things have to be.'

'I'll keep trying,' Frank Waverly said, no longer appearing as confident as he had before.

Looking around, Matt asked, 'What did you do with the dead?'

'Threw them in the river — they're on their way to the Gulf of Mexico.' At Matt's disapproving frown, Frank asked, 'Did you want to scrape out graves for them with your hands and hold a Christian burial?'

'No. I'm sorry, Frank. It just seems . . . worse somehow.'

'Worse than leaving them on the beach to decay and feed the carrion birds?' Frank responded. The man was obviously wound up tightly, but Matt did not think it was over the dead men. Serenity watched their conversation from horseback.

'You did all you could, Frank,' Matt said. 'Let's see how much traveling we can get done before sunset.'

They unsaddled the horses the land pirates had been riding and set them free. They would find their way back to Camelback eventually, and perhaps would serve to caution any other man with big ideas.

They rode from the river course and onto the empty prairie land once more. The sun was lowering in the west, dropping slowly behind the peaks of the Guadalupe Mountains. Travel would become difficult after dark, even knowing the land as they did. Neither Serenity nor Frank Waverly would make it home this night.

As the sun sketched long shadows out beneath their horses, they came within sight of an oak grove where fifty or so trees stood alone atop a low knoll.

'We may as well make camp there,' Frank said, and Matt agreed. It would be a cold, hungry night, but the horses would have graze and with the morning sun they would be rested enough to continue on their way.

The oak trees offered some shelter from the wind which continued to drive across the prairie, and they spread their bedrolls on the dry earth of the copse. Matt had taken the saddle-bags containing the gold from his horse's back as Serenity watched with sharply assessing eyes. He folded them as a rough pillow to place beneath his head. It was no time to take chances with the money.

Matt slept fitfully. Despite his two blankets, the night was cold. His pillow, valued at $20,000 wasn't worth a one-dollar down pillow as far as comfort went. From time to time Serenity and Frank both stirred, rose and disappeared into the shadows. But their movements were not furtive. No one made a move toward Matt's bed.

Dawn arrived with suddenness. Orange light colored the sky and spears of light shafted through the trees. A flock of crows had taken refuge in the trees as night had fallen. Now they were suddenly taking to wing, as if the sun had disturbed their sleep.

The sun, or the man who entered the camp with his rifle trained on their beds.

11

Serenity sat up sharply with a little gasp. Frank Waverly opened his eyes slowly, then they narrowed with anger. They all recognized the man holding them at gunpoint.

'Did you think I was that easy to get rid of, Frank?' Whiskey Pete asked. 'After all the time we spent together, you should know me better.'

'What are you after, Pete?' Frank asked. He shifted in his bed and Pete told him:

'Sit still, Frank. I like having you just where you are. The same goes for you,' he said to Matt. The short man's beard had grown some. He hadn't paused to get a shave in Camelback.

Pete said, 'Why wouldn't I be here, Frank? That gold cost me four years of my life. What did I get for my troubles?' He nodded at Serenity, 'First that little she-cat locks me in a cellar, and when you show up are you willing to do the right thing by me? The hell! You toss me ten dollars like I was some street bum and chase me off.

'That was wrong, Frank, dead wrong. We all had a cut of the money coming. We were all in on it together. We all did prison time for it. But you — you — are the only one who comes out of it alive and with gold in your pockets. I never took you for that kind of man.'

'If you'd let me explain . . . ' Frank Waverly said, shifting again in his bed, a movement which did not go unnoticed by Whiskey Pete.

'Explain what! That you turned your back on your old partners and hogged the gold.'

'We can still split it up, Pete.' Frank Waverly was obviously playing for time.

'No, we can't, Frank,' Pete said. 'You had your chance to play it straight, and you didn't. Why should I play straight with you? Where is it?' he demanded, cocking his rifle.

'It's here,' Matt volunteered, to give Frank a moment to shift his hand closer to his pistol. Standing, hands held high, Matt toed the saddlebags which gave off an unmistakable clinking sound.

'I'll be taking those,' Pete said. 'You back up.'

Matt stepped backward a few paces, still holding his hands high. A tight little smile played across Whiskey Pete's lips. He kept his rifle trained loosely on Frank Waverly, but now Pete was forced to bend down and hoist the heavy saddle-bags, his eyes on the gold and on the nearby Matt Holiday.

Serenity moved. Frank twisted in his blankets.

Whiskey Pete fired wildly in Frank's direction as the outlaw got to his knees in his bed and drew his Colt. A .44 bullet from Waverly's Colt tagged Pete at the base of his throat. Blood flowed from his mouth and he pitched forward on his face, to lie motionless in the dust.

It was over before Matt Holiday

could blink twice. Frank Waverly was rising to his feet, smoke curling from the muzzle of his gun. His victim lay motionless, rifle fallen from his hand. Frank turned his head to say something to Serenity, but she had fallen onto her back. The shot from Pete's Winchester had taken her full in the chest.

Frank and Matt both rushed to her, but there was no stanching the blood. It flowed freely, staining her white blouse to deep maroon. Her eyes were open, but she seemed to see nothing. Her lips trembled and moved, but no sound emerged.

Matt remained on his knees beside her, silent in the light of the new dawn as Frank Waverly rose and walked to where Whiskey Pete lay. Frank drew his boot back and kicked the body savagely. He stood over Pete's body for a long while, his chest rising and falling with emotion. Then he walked back to where his dead daughter lay, holstering his gun.

'Let's get them over to the river,' Frank Waverly said. He crouched and picked Serenity up in his arms, giving her one last tender kiss.

The ride to the river was somber, silent. Matt wanted to speak, but could think of nothing suitable. He could not ease Frank Waverly's grief; there was no longer any point in cursing at Whiskey Pete.

So many people had died for want of this gold, and not one of them had gained a thing in pursuing it.

They slipped the bodies, one at a time into the river current and watched as they were swept away. Frank watched after Serenity until she was carried around a bend in the river and there was nothing left to see. The river flowed on, uncaring. The day grew warmer.

'Well?' Matt asked at last when Frank seemed unwilling or unable to move. 'Do you want to go by your house and tell Bertha what happened?'

Waverly did not look at him. He shook his head heavily and answered, 'I don't think I'm ready to face my wife just yet, Matt. What do you say we ford the river and head west directly to El Paso? Deliver the gold to Butterfield. At least I'll have that off my mind.'

And so they did, splashing across the river, leading Serenity's sorrel which now carried the saddle-bags filled with gold. By nightfall they had reached El Paso, spoken to Warren Petty and placed the gold in his safe at the Butterfield office.

Frank Waverly watched dispassionately as Petty had an official letter written and notarized by the county clerk and asked that a copy be sent off to the prison warden. 'You're clear now, Waverly. You're a free man, but,' Petty warned him, 'don't ever get back in the business again.'

'Why would I? I'm not going through anything like this ever again.'

'What's wrong with him?' Petty asked Holiday as Matt lingered in his office, leaving Waverly to hunt down a hotel room. 'I thought he'd be a little happier.'

Matt told Petty what had happened,

or at least a part of it. It now seemed so long ago, far away and confused. They spent a few minutes discussing company business, then, with a yawn, Petty rose and shook Matt's hand.

'Last time?' Petty asked.

'I think so, Warren. I'll let you know for sure when I get back.'

* * *

There was little talking between the two men as they started east once more. Frank rode as if under a cloud of angry despair. One noon, while they let their horses drink from a pond formed by the passing rain, the outlaw did say:

'It was all my fault, wasn't it, Matt? Serenity, that is. I gave her no sort of guidance.'

Matt, crouched beside his horse as it drank, looked up and said seriously, 'I don't know, Frank. I'm sure that must have been a part of it, but then again, look at Laura. As I understand it, Ben Kennedy was as much of an outlaw as you were, and it seems she's turned out just fine.' Musing, he added, 'I wonder where she is now?'

'Still at my place, I'd imagine,' Frank said. 'She told me that she was going to take Will there and then wait.'

'Wait? For what?'

'You'd have to ask her,' Frank Waverly said, swinging into the saddle once more.

The sky was clear and hot when they first glimpsed the small collection of adobes that was Bentley, Texas. The river flowed easily past the pecan grove where Matt's involvement with the Waverlys had begun. The wind sifted fine dust over them. Waverly drew up his horse and looked down on the tiny settlement.

'It's not much, is it?' Frank asked.

'How much does a man need?'

Frank did not answer. Matt knew that Waverly was less than eager to ride home and tell his wife what had happened. It certainly wasn't the kind of homecoming he was used to or had expected this to be.

'Are you coming?' the outlaw asked Matt.

'No.' The two — man and wife — had their grief to attend to. Now was not the time to be a visitor.

'All right,' Frank nodded. 'Back in El Paso, when you and Petty were alone talking, did that have something to do with me?'

'No. It was just business, that's all. They've been asking me for some time to move up to the office and take a desk job. Now I think it's time at last. I seem to be ready for it.'

'Had enough of the long trail, have you?'

'I think so, yes. I think maybe it's time for the both of us to quit it once and for all.'

Frank nodded. Briefly he placed a hand on Matt's shoulder. 'Come by later, if you have a mind to.'

Then the outlaw rode off on the little palomino toward the small house where a woman was waiting. Matt wished them both well. He watched until Frank had splashed across the river and made his way up the narrow trail toward his house, then he started the buckskin forward again.

In the shade of the pecan grove it was still warm despite the shadows cast by the trees. Matt Holiday looked across the river, seeing Will Waverly. With him was Laura Kennedy, her boots off, her skirt hiked up as she laughed and waded into the river, returning with a ten-pound catfish, delighting Will. Laughing, Laura dropped the wriggling fish into their bucket and sat down on the grass. Laura laughed, mussing Will's hair. Her own red tresses had fallen free, burnished to gold by the sunlight.

They both were free of their own prisons now, it seemed. Matt Holiday watched them for a few more minutes, then swung into the saddle once more. Crossing the river as the two looked up in pleased surprise, Matt found himself wondering what it would be like to be married to an outlaw's daughter.

We do hope that you have enjoyed reading this large print book.

Did you know that all of our titles are available for purchase?

We publish a wide range of high quality large print books including:
Romances, Mysteries, Classics
General Fiction
Non Fiction and Westerns

Special interest titles available in large print are:
The Little Oxford Dictionary
Music Book, Song Book
Hymn Book, Service Book

Also available from us courtesy of Oxford University Press:
Young Readers' Dictionary
(large print edition)
Young Readers' Thesaurus
(large print edition)

For further information or a free brochure, please contact us at:
Ulverscroft Large Print Books Ltd.,
The Green, Bradgate Road, Anstey,
Leicester, LE7 7FU, England.
Tel: (00 44) **0116 236 4325**
Fax: (00 44) **0116 234 0205**

LADY COLT

Steve Hayes

When word comes through that two of the infamous Wallace brothers have been spotted in Indian Territory, Liberty Mercer — only the second woman ever to become a Deputy US Marshal — rides out to arrest them. But things don't go to plan, and Liberty finds herself left in the desert to die. Fortunately, rescue comes in the unlikely shape of a young girl named Clementina, on the run herself — from a stepmother who happens to be the matriarch of the Wallace gang . . .

THE GHOSTS OF POYNTER

Amos Carr

Chase Tyler is headed for the town of Poynter. An attempted ambush, the death of an innocent man and a sheriff who won't play by the rules, added to a brother-in-law who can't be trusted and a young man out for vengeance, all make for a pretty complicated visit. When Chase also meets a woman who bears more than a passing resemblance to his lost love, it would seem there is very little hope of him laying old ghosts to rest . . .

STOP OLLINGER!

Jack Dakota

When the town of Mud Wagon Creek is destroyed by desperadoes, it is just the start of a twisted trail of revenge for outlaw-boss Bass Ollinger. He has sworn to make society pay for the time he spent in the Oregon State Penitentiary, and he intends to blaze a trail of death and destruction clear from Texas to the Beaver State . . . Riding the border country, Brant Forrest unwittingly rides into Ollinger's path, and comes to the inevitable conclusion: stop Ollinger!

ACE OF BONES

Clay Starmer

When famed gunslinger Reno Valance rides out, the instructions are clear: collect his wife's relative and return home. But for the man who used to be known as Ace, it turns out not to be so simple: Uncle Gifford is dead — murdered! Soon a world of evil is unleashed, and Reno is forced to make a decision. He's dealt the devil's card for twenty years, and now he'll have to do it once more, taking up his Remington as the Ace of Bones . . .

BEYOND REDEMPTION

I. J. Parnham

As a child, Jeff Dale witnesses the terrible aftermath of an atrocity: Elmer Drake has killed three members of a family, but the daughter, Cynthia, is missing. Jeff vows that he'll find her, no matter how long it takes. Years later, after finding a clue about Cynthia's fate, Jeff follows the trail to the frontier town of Redemption. Here stalks a man who carries a gun in one hand and a cross in the other. A man called Elmer Drake . . .

PRAISE BE TO SILVER

Ethan Flagg

Framed for the killing of an assay agent in the Colorado town of Green Ridge, Morgan Silver escapes the lethal attentions of a vigilante mob by the skin of his teeth. With his new identity he heads south, but fate in the shape of the real killer appears, and thwarts his every move. Fortunately, Lady Luck steps in once again to aid the fugitive — but he will need nerves of steel and a steady hand to clear his name . . .